*Also by Ruth White*

SWEET CREEK HOLLER

# WEEPING WILLOW

RUTH WHITE

# Weeping Willow

Farrar, Straus and Giroux New York

*To Garnet, Gipsy, Roberta, and Vicky,*
*and to the Grundy High School Class of 1960*

# WEEPING WILLOW

*When I was a baby and still close to the other side where we're all from, Willa was there. I don't remember not knowing her. While I was learning to walk and talk, she came and went freely, and I never thought to question who she might be. I remember her voice was like a bell, and when she laughed she covered her face with her hands and peeped out between her fingers. As I got older, Willa appeared only when I called her:*

> Willa, Willa, on my pilla',
> Come in your pretty lace
> And your pink face.

*Then she would come and play with me. She had curly red hair and her eyes changed color with the weather. On bright days they were green, on rainy days they were* blue, and when it snowed they were gray like the sky. Oh, she smelled good! And she wore the frilliest feminine finery.

What I didn't know about Willa as we grew up together was that nobody could see her but me.

"Who're you talking to, Tiny?" Mama sometimes asked.

"Willa."

"Who's Willa?"

I thought she was fooling. "Oh, Mama, you know Willa."

And Mama, being like she was, wasn't interested enough to go on with it.

It was when I started school that I ran into trouble with Willa. There was a cloakroom between the first and second grades where my teacher, Mrs. Skeens, made us go and sit alone when we misbehaved. I spent a lot of time in the cloakroom, but I didn't mind because Willa came to keep me company. We played counting games on our fingers, and whispered secrets and nursery rhymes.

Then one day Willa told me a funny story that made me laugh out loud, and Mrs. Skeens came into the cloakroom.

"What's so funny, Tiny?" she asked.

"Willa told me a joke."

"Who is Willa?"

There was that question again.

"Oh, you know Willa," I said, just like I had to Mama.

But Mrs. Skeens didn't give up. She put her hands on her hips and said, "No, I do not know Willa, and I want you to tell me about her right now."

*So I told her, and that was a big mistake. Mrs. Skeens did not like Willa at all.*

*"Tiny Lambert," she said. "That is about the silliest piece of nonsense I ever heard, and if that good-for-nothing mama of yours never told you, let me be the one to inform you, there is no Willa! She is not real, understand? She is just a figment of your imagination."*

*I was surprised at Mrs. Skeens. Why, anybody with eyes could see Willa a mile away with that red hair. She most certainly was not a figment.*

*Then I remembered how Mama questioned me about Willa, and I thought of the times I talked to Willa on the playground, and the other children looked at me funny. For the first time I wondered . . . and when I turned to look at Willa, she was gone. Only a whiff of her good smell stayed behind.*

*For days I tried to call her back.*

Willa, Willa, on my pilla' . . .

*But she was gone, and I cried.*

*I guess Mrs. Skeens did what she did for my own good, but I couldn't stand her after that.*

*Still, I always felt Willa was near me somewhere— just around a corner, or in the shadows at twilight, and someday, if and when I really needed her, she would come to me again.*

# ONE

> I rolled over and opened my eyes and a sudden thrill went through me. It was like the rush you get in the movies when the cavalry comes charging over the horizon blowing their bugles to save the settlers. Something wonderful was going to happen today. I could feel it.

It was real early on my first day of high school in the fall of 1956. I got up, careful not to wake my half sister, Phyllis, and tiptoed out into the hall, and into the bathroom. Nobody could have heard me, but as soon as I started running water the whole house came alive. The next thing I knew, Vern, my stepfather, was pounding on the bathroom door, telling me to get a move on. Then Beau and Luther, my half brothers, who were trying to act like their daddy, did the same thing.

I hurried back to the bedroom, where Phyllis turned over in our big double bed, mumbled something, and hit the floor. She wandered downstairs, where Mama was fixing breakfast for everybody. Mama always did that on the first day of school to show her good intentions. When we were gone, she could go back to sleep, undisturbed, for the first time in three months.

I had my school clothes neatly laid out on a chair— a dark plaid dress with a straight skirt, and black-and-white saddle oxfords with bobby sox. I slipped a pair of shorts on under my dress because I had absolutely no hips at all, and the shorts rounded me out some.

Then I took the bobby pins out of my brown hair and brushed curls around my face, dabbed on a bit of lipstick and compact makeup, and stood back to look at myself in the mirror. I saw no chance of ever being beautiful. First of all, I was too small. I weighed only ninety-five pounds after a long drink of water, and I was only five feet tall in thick soles. My complexion was kinda sallow and my eyes pale blue, like Mama's. I was plain, and that's all there was to it.

I put my perfectly pink lipstick into my genuine plastic pocketbook along with my compact. Then I picked up my five-subject composition notebook and two number-two pencils, and I was ready for high school.

Downstairs, Mama had made pancakes and sausages. As we sat there all crowded around the table with the smell of coffee and the clatter of dishes, it was like we were a real family as normal as any other. Only I knew better.

My own daddy, who was not married to my mama, had gone off to the war in Europe in December 1941, and was never heard from again. Five months after he left, I was born on the top of Ruby Mountain.

Then, when I was three years old, Vernon Mullins, a coal miner for the Ruby Valley Coal Company, started courting my mama. Her daddy, my Grandpa Lambert, nearly had a fit because he said there had been bad blood between the Lamberts and the Mullinses for a hundred years. No, he didn't remember why, but he knew there was a good reason for it, and if Mama persisted in marrying that no-account Mullins, then she'd better take me and everything she owned—all of which could fit in a paper poke—and never darken his doorway on Ruby Mountain again.

So she did. And I hadn't seen Grandpa Lambert since.

Mama and Vern got married, and the two of us moved into Vern's house down here in Ruby Valley. Now, you would think with such a pretty name, the place would have to be a real jewel, but Ruby Valley was only a holler, and a holler is nothing more than a glorified gully between two mountains. There was a creek and a road side by side, both of which ran to the head of the holler and Ruby Mountain. The road ended right up there at Grandpa Lambert's place.

Vern's house was a big, shabby thing with a bathroom, which was a new convenience for me and Mama.

The house was left to Vern by his grandfather, who had built it but never really finished it right. The floorboards in the hall and bedrooms upstairs were still raw lumber, and you could get splinters in your feet if you weren't careful. One time Vern decided to put in a whole new fireplace in the living room. He tore out all the old bricks and hauled them off. Then he bought all new bricks and stacked them by the hole in the wall. There they had stayed for years.

The house just hung on the hill with a skinny dirt road, edged by a rock wall leading up to it, and ending under a high porch on stilts. Vern parked his pickup truck under that tall porch.

When Mama and I moved in, Vern was working third shift in the mines, which meant he worked nights and slept days. Mama always had been a night owl herself, and pretty soon she was staying up all night, too, and sleeping during the day with Vern. I spent more and more time alone, and had to be quiet so Mama and Vern could sleep. To pass the time, I called Willa to me and we would play. She taught me to count and to sing—softly.

Mama cooked one meal a day, and that was supper. I ate with Mama and Vern, then I'd go to bed. I don't know what Mama did all night while Vern was at work. One time I went downstairs to get a drink of water and I saw her sitting in the dark smoking a cigarette.

When Vern started working days, Mama couldn't break her old habits. She went to bed very late, and got up and fixed Vern's breakfast if he made her; then she went back to bed. She still cooked only one big meal in the evenings. Other than that she did very little. It didn't take a grownup person to figure out my mama was awful unhappy.

Then the stairstep babies started coming. First there was Beau when I was five, then Luther a year later, and Phyllis a year after that. Those babies wouldn't cooperate with Mama to save your life. They never ate or slept when she wanted them to, so she had to stay awake, and she was real grouchy. After school, on weekends, and in the summertime, she tried to make me mind the babies, but most of the time I couldn't make them hush, so Mama had to stumble around, half-asleep, and tend them her own self.

It seemed everybody in our house was either grumbling or blubbering, and that's when I missed Willa the most. But Mrs. Skeens had taken her away from me.

Vern grew fat and drank more than his share. I don't think he and Mama even liked each other anymore. The only person Vern would turn a hand for was Phyllis. He showered her with attention, and she was spoiled rotten.

But that first day of school, when I was fourteen, everybody seemed to be in a good mood for a change. Vern was teasing the boys about not recognizing them with their faces clean, and he was bouncing Phyllis— "Daddy's little girl"—on his knee. Beau was nine and just entering the fourth grade. Luther was eight and in the third, and Phyllis was seven and in the second.

Vern turned to me and looked me over good.

"Well, Tiny, now you're going to be a high school

girl, and a pretty one, too. Just don't get too big for your britches."

I managed a smile.

"Me and Hazel never had a chance to go to high school, you know."

"How come?" I said, though I had heard this one a dozen times.

" 'Cause I had to go to work when I was thirteen, and your mama lived up on that mountaintop. It was too far to the high school, and they didn't have buses back then. You're a lucky girl."

He went on talking about how hard things were in the old days, and how easy I had it, but I wasn't listening. My mind was racing ahead into the day. What would high school be like? Would my teachers be real mean? Would I make friends this year? I never had before. Every kid in Ruby Valley Grade School had known me and I had a reputation for being a loner. Maybe this year, with a larger school and all those strangers, things would be different.

Vern left for work and the kids went back upstairs to finish dressing and get their stuff together. Their bus would come later than mine. Mama and I were alone at the table.

"You really do look pretty, Tiny," she said.

I was surprised. She smiled a sad kind of smile. She was only thirty, but she had bags under her eyes, and she was thin and small like me.

"Thanks," I mumbled, blushing.

I was trying to finish a cup of coffee just because I thought it was a grownup thing to do. I really didn't like it.

"And you remember one thing, girl," Mama went on.

She never could leave well enough alone.

"You're just as good as any of them—better than most. Don't let anybody tell you any different."

I knew she was trying to be nice, but that bit of advice made me mad. I had almost talked myself into thinking I could make friends this year till then. What made her think about saying that? Maybe it was because I really wasn't as good as the rest, and maybe I didn't look pretty either.

"I gotta go!" I said, and left the table abruptly.

I was out the door and on my way down the hill before she could do any more damage.

# TWO

It was a perfect September morning. The sky was a still blue above the hills, where some of the trees were just beginning to turn. I could smell smoke, and bacon frying somewhere.

Cecil Hess was down by the roadside, the first as always, waiting for the bus.

"Hey, Cecil," I said breathlessly.

"Hey, Tiny," he said and grinned at me.

Cecil was one of those boys everybody liked. You couldn't help it. He was friendly and good-natured, with freckles and a turned-up nose. He made you laugh, and he was dependable. In the last year he had shot up a head taller than me.

"I was so excited I was up at 5 a.m.," he said, laughing. "I saw the sun come up."

That was another thing about Cecil—he was an open book. You knew you could trust him because what he thought he said. What other boy would admit to looking forward to the first day of high school?

Cecil and I had grown up together and we were used to each other in a brother-sister kind of way, but you couldn't call us friends because he was a boy. We had missed only one year being in the same room at school, which was the previous year, and that was because I took beginner's band and Cecil didn't. I played the clarinet. Mr. Stewart, the county band director, came to our school every day to give us music lessons, and the eighth-grade band members had to be in the same room.

Cecil lived across the road and the creek with his parents and four little brothers and sisters. Next door to them were the Combs family. Beside our house on the hillside lived the Horns. Behind us, farther up the hill, was Aunt Evie Delong's shack, and closer to the road on our side were the Boyds. These six houses in a cluster made up our neighborhood here in the bend. There were plenty of other houses scattered throughout the holler, but no more in sight of us.

The high school bus appeared around the bend. Mrs. Stacy, the driver, waved as she drove by. She would go up the holler first, then pick us up on the way back down.

J. C. Combs, Dolly Horn, and Joyce Boyd came out of their houses and joined us at the bus stop. They were all seniors, and they talked about things like guidance counselors and class rings. Cecil and I felt inferior, so we didn't say anything.

Directly, the bus came back down the road and stopped for us. We climbed aboard and I glanced around quickly at the girls. I groaned because nobody else had on a plaid dress or saddle oxfords. They were wearing skirts and blouses and white bucks. Last year, when I was still in brown lace-ups, they had saddle oxfords. So I got me a pair of saddle oxfords, and now they were sporting white bucks! How did they know these things? Nobody ever said, "Hey, let's get together and buy white bucks." No, it just happened by instinct or something, and I was the one who never was tuned in.

Cecil and I settled down in a back seat, perfectly still, but taking in everything.

After making frequent stops to pick up more students, we left the mouth of Ruby Valley and went over a big steel bridge and onto the main highway, which followed the river into Black Gap. The whole trip took about twenty minutes.

Black Gap High School was a large two-story redbrick building with a white steeple over the front entrance. Behind it the hills rose dark against the sky.

Mrs. Stacy told us to go to the auditorium for instructions. I was grateful for Cecil's presence. Together we found the auditorium, where sheets of paper were tacked along the wall listing the homerooms and who was in them. They were done alphabetically, so that once again Cecil and I were assigned to the same room.

We followed the white bucks down the black-and-

white-tiled hallway and found the right place—Mrs.
Yates's homeroom. There we settled in again and
watched and listened and waited.

Some of our classmates from Ruby Valley were
there, along with many strange faces from other hol-
lers, and of course the town kids dominated everything.

Mrs. Yates gave us our schedules for the year. I was
to have English, algebra, history, science, home ec.,
and band. I could hang on to Cecil most of the day,
since his schedule was the same as mine until fifth
period, when he had shop instead of home ec. Then
sixth period he had phys. ed. and I had band.

That first day we spent only thirty minutes in each
class, being introduced to our teachers and the subject
matter. I tried to take careful notes, but by third period
it occurred to me that all the teachers were saying the
same things I had heard for eight years in a row. Maybe
they were just like me—all fired up the first day, then
gradually fizzling out by the end of the week, making
the rest of the school year just as boring as every other
year.

Fifth period, I followed a strange girl to the home
ec. room when I heard her say she was going there,
and after that Judy Snead, a band girl from Ruby
Valley, helped me find the band room.

That's when my whole life changed. I didn't know
it right away, but that's when it happened—that very
moment when I stepped into the band room. It was a
very large room on the second floor overlooking a
graveyard smack on the hill outside the window.
Around the room were semicircles of chairs and music
stands clustered around a podium on a platform front

and center. That's where Mr. Stewart would stand and direct. Each section of the room was labeled—wood-winds, percussion, brass. I settled down in the wood-winds section. I didn't see the band director come in and take his place on the platform because other students were milling around me. But when my section was seated, and I looked up, it was *not* pudgy little Mr. Stewart I saw—oh no. Here was a creature wonderful in proportion and appeal—a joy to behold right there in front of me. He was tall, tan, blond, and blue-eyed, but it was his marvelous arms that held me spellbound. With a baton in one hand, the arms were raised, perfectly poised. Did I say he had blond hairs on his arms? Well, he did. Then he lowered those arms and tapped the baton on his music stand.

"Attention please," was all he said.

And he had us in his back pocket.

"I am Mr. Gillespie."

He did not talk like people in Black Gap, Virginia. He did not move like somebody who grew up in a holler, and I could not picture him as the son of a coal miner. You could be sure he was from elsewhere—Hollywood, California, maybe.

"I am your band director. As you probably know, Mr. Stewart resigned during the summer. I am a recent graduate of the University of Virginia, and I feel very fortunate to be here with you."

Then he smiled.

I snapped a photo of that smile into my brain so that, afterward, I could close my eyes and see him standing there with his golden arms, smiling down at us.

The girl beside me giggled and poked me.

"He's cute," she whispered, and I glanced at her briefly.

She was petite, blond, and green-eyed.

"I'm Bobby Lynn Clevinger," she said.

But I was lost in Mr. Gillespie's spell. Already I had forgotten Bobby Lynn Clevinger.

"What's your name?" she insisted, poking me again.

"Tiny Lambert," I said, irritated.

"I mean your real name," she came back.

"Tiny Lambert!"

"We have to play for all the football games," Mr. Gillespie was saying. "So we have to practice on the field. Starting tomorrow, you must bring your instruments every day."

"Tiny is not a name; it's an adjective," Bobby Lynn whispered.

"And Bobby is a boy's name!" I shot back.

She giggled again.

"It's short for Roberta. So what's Tiny short for? Teenie Weenie? Little Bitty?"

That was the first but far from the last time Bobby Lynn started me giggling in band.

"So where do you live, Little Bitty?" Bobby Lynn teased me after we left the band room.

"Ruby Valley. Where do you live?"

"In town."

And that was the final remarkable event of that most remarkable half hour when I was giggling with a town girl while falling in love with a god.

# THREE

⌐ Climbing up the hill to home after getting off the bus was always the worst part of the school day. But since that day had been only three hours long, I was home by twelve forty-five, and I practically ran up the hill. That was a big mistake because when I got to the porch steps I ran smack into them and bumped my shins. I was always doing stupid things like that.

I rubbed my legs and glanced around to see if anybody was looking at me, and right next door, in the Horns' fenced-in front yard, was the most beautiful collie dog I ever saw. I about fainted because I'd always wanted a collie, and Vern wouldn't let me have a dog at all. I walked around and knelt beside the fence.

"Hey, boy," I whispered to him and put my fingers through the wire.

He wagged his tail and came to me. I can't tell you how much I loved that dog!

"It's a girl," Dolly said as she entered her yard.

"She's so pretty, Dolly. What's her name?"

"Tennessee, 'cause that's where she came from. We call her Nessie for short."

"Is she yours?"

"Yeah."

Nessie kept looking at me and made no move to go to Dolly. Dolly went inside.

"If you were mine, Nessie," I said, "you would never leave my side."

Nessie grinned.

After a while I reluctantly left the dog and went into my own house. The kids were eating cold beans and light bread. I poured myself a glass of buttermilk.

"So how was school?" I said to nobody in particular as I parked myself at the table.

"Awful," from Beau.

"Stupid," from Luther.

"Miz Matney don't like me," from Phyllis.

"Already?" from me.

"Nobody likes you," from Beau.

"Daddy does," from Phyllis.

"Daddy does," Luther mimicked her.

"Oh, shut up, Luther," Phyllis said.

Luther cracked Phyllis on the head with his knuckles and she started bawling.

"Holy cow," I said in disgust. "Can't y'all get along for five minutes?"

I put my dirty glass in the sink with the breakfast dishes.

"Look who's so high and mighty since she's in high school!" Beau said.

I ignored him.

"Luther's a nasty old . . ." Phyllis struggled to find the right word. ". . . slop jar!" she bellowed at last.

"A what?" Beau, Luther, and I said together.

"A nasty old slop jar!" Phyllis cried.

That set the rest of us to laughing.

"A nasty old slop jar, huh?" I said. "Well, let's get him, what d'you say?"

"Yeah!" Phyllis smiled through her tears, and we all made a dive for Luther.

The floor was covered with a roll-down linoleum rug, and it was sticky and grimy, but that's where we were rasslin', tickling Luther, squealing, and giggling, when Mama's voice cut through the din. I wondered what she was doing up and with a dress on, too.

"What's all this racket?" she said crossly.

Of course we didn't pay her any attention. We never did. She grumbled and went to the sink. She filled it full of hot, soapy water, acting like she was going to do the dishes.

We stopped playing and settled around the table again.

"You can just do the dishes, Miss Smarty," Mama said to me. "Since all you have to do is waller on the floor."

I went to the sink without a word. Syrup and grease were congealed on the plates. Oh well, she did cook breakfast, and in all fairness to Mama, she rarely made me do the work she hated to do herself.

Mama turned on the electric stove to heat up the morning coffee, which had grown strong enough to stand alone. Then she sat down at the table.

"The telephone company's coming at two," she said.

"The telephone company!" we chorused.

So that's why Mama was up and dressed.

"Yeah, they said if we could get everybody in the bend to join a party line, they'd run us a pole up here."

"And are they all going in?" I said.

"Yeah, all except Aunt Evie. We're meeting at the Hesses'."

"You mean it?"

"Yeah," Mama said, pleased with herself. "I mean it."

"We don't know nobody to call," Beau said.

I went on washing dishes and looked out at the hills against the sky. My mind was racing through the next four years of high school. Bobby Lynn Clevinger probably had a telephone. All the town kids did. Maybe she would call me, and maybe a boy would call me.

"Mama, can I have a pair of white bucks?"

"A pair of what?"

"White bucks. They're shoes. And everybody—"

"And what's wrong with your saddle oxfords is what I'd like to know?"

"Oh, I love my saddle oxfords, but if I had two pairs of shoes for school, they wouldn't wear out so fast, see?"

"No, I don't see, and I'll tell you one thing right

now, you can just get this new-shoes disease out of your system. I'll not hear no more about it."

The coffee began to perk, and she poured herself a cup. I finished the dishes.

"Now, go see if Aunt Evie wants anything from the A & P," Mama said.

"Are we going to the A & P?"

"Yeah, when Vern comes home."

We went to the A & P about every two or three weeks because they had so much more stuff than the small coal company store down the holler.

I went out the back door, which opened onto the hillside, and I turned to the right and followed a well-worn path that curved around the hill to Aunt Evie's shack above us.

Aunt Evie was nobody's aunt that I knew of, but everybody called her that. She was sixty-three and just as poor as you can possibly be and still exist. She had no known income whatsoever. She couldn't even take in washing because she had no washing machine and no well. Once in a while she did some sewing and canning for people, but that was about it. That's why our community pitched in and gave her things all the time, like coal in winter. Every time any of us went to the store, we picked up something for her, too, like cornmeal, or beans, or lard. And always when you took it to her, she said, "I don't have no change right now. I'll pay you later."

"Okay," we said.

She owed us about a thousand dollars apiece, but nobody was counting, because everybody loved Aunt

Evie. Like Cecil, she was the kind of person you naturally loved.

When Aunt Evie was a young girl of seventeen and dressed up in white at the church, she was jilted. She never got over it; in fact, she talked about it almost every day these forty-six years later. She was always laying plans for "when Ward comes back . . ." She was convinced that something prevented him from showing at the church that day, and she still expected him to return to her. Even though Ward had disappeared from these parts altogether and never contacted Aunt Evie again, she never gave up hope. When she had candles on winter nights she burned them in the windows for Ward. In the summer she sat out on her tiny porch and watched every car that came up the holler. She was pitiful.

But every person I knew, adult or child, visited Aunt Evie. She listened to you, and she remembered everything you said to her. She never judged or shamed you, and you always left her feeling like you had solved something.

I knocked on her door, then walked in, because in the first place, I knew she was home. Where else would she be? And in the second place, nobody in Ruby Valley ever locked a door. It was such a bother to have to stop whatever it was you were doing to unlock it when somebody came.

Aunt Evie's house was very small and dark. It used to be a miner's shack a hundred years ago, and it still looked the same as it did then. There were two rooms—a sitting room and kitchen together, and a small bedroom tucked right into the hillside in back. There was a side door leading to a huge clearing in the woods which served as her back yard.

"Hidy, girl," she greeted me.

She was eating boiled potatoes at the kitchen table.

"Pull up a cheer and have a tater."

I sat down with her.

"No thanks, Aunt Evie. Mama says you need anything from the store?"

"I'd like to have me some brown sugar if hit's not a bother to you."

"Anything else?"

"Not today, honey. How was school?"

"Okay. I made a friend, Aunt Evie."

"First day? That's good, Tiny."

So I told her about Bobby Lynn Clevinger.

"Clevingers are good folks," she said. "Is she Jacob's girl or Horace's girl?"

"I didn't ask her daddy's name."

"If she's Horace's girl, she's got the finest daddy ever lived and breathed. Horace's daddy, Clint, was Ward's good friend."

I leaned in close in the dim room and whispered, "Guess what, Aunt Evie?"

She wiped a bit of potato from the corner of her mouth and grinned.

"Hit's a boy, ain't hit?"

"No, it's a teacher," I said, giggling. "It's our new band director, Mr. Gillespie. It was love at first sight."

"So tell me," she said breathlessly, like she was interested and excited for me, and I believe she really was. She hung on to every word I said, and asked me to repeat the part about the blond hairs on his arms. She liked that. Pretty soon she was giggling with me.

"Tiny's in love! Tiny's in love!" she chanted like a schoolgirl.

"Oh, Aunt Evie, nobody's ever going to love the likes of me."

"And what do you mean by the likes of you? You're about as fine as they come."

"Oh, you know, I'm not pretty and popular. I never know what to wear. Everybody else seems to know. And I don't know what to say to boys. I'm always daydreaming, and I run into things, and—"

"My goodness," Aunt Evie interrupted me. "I'm sure glad you told me how awful you are. 'Cause if you hadn't a'told me, Tiny Lambert, I woulda thought you's an all-right gal. But I reckon you orta know."

"You know what I mean, Aunt Evie."

"I know you sell yourself short. Just keep telling yourself how bad you are, and sure enough you'll live up to your own expectations."

"What d'you mean?"

"Have you got time for a story?"

"Sure."

I always loved Aunt Evie's stories.

"Well, I knowed this family when I was a girl of twenty. They were smart enough, I reckon, and good folks, too, but ugly! Whoo—ee! They were nearabout the ugliest people I ever saw. They all had tiny, squinty eyes set real close together, humped noses, and big elongated chins. It was embarrassing to see them all out together. Folks looked away. Well, poor Lila was my age and probably the ugliest one of the bunch, but the tenderest-hearted. Hit hurt her real bad not to have one spark of good looks to her name. She nearly cried her eyes out before Clyde Justus come along, twenty years older'n her, and no looker hisself, but a good man, and he took her to wed. In a year's time, Lila found herself with child, and confided to me, as I was her onliest friend.

" 'Evie,' she said to me. 'My baby's going to be the loveliest child ever seed in these parts.'

"I said, 'Course hit will be, Lila.'

"I honestly didn't see how Lila and Clyde could have a pretty child. But, Tiny, I was wrong and I learned a valuable lesson."

"You mean they did have a pretty baby?"

"Yeah, the most adorable little girl, who grew up into the most beautiful woman ever I beheld. Hit was a pleasure just to look at her."

"How do you explain it, Aunt Evie?"

"Why, hit's easy, honey. From the day that child was conceived, she heard only good things said about herself. Her mother talked to her constantly before and after she was born.

" 'You are beautiful. You are remarkable,' Lila would say to the child. 'You are my bright and shining star. You have silken curls, big sparkling eyes, a rosy complexion,' things like that all the time. You know, she actually shaped that child."

I sat in silence, thinking about her story.

"You see," she went on, "we come to believe what we tell ourselfs over and over, and hit's our beliefs that shape things."

Could it be true?

"Well, that's something to think about, Aunt Evie," I said.

"You're a smart girl, Tiny," Aunt Evie said and grinned. She had teeth missing all over the place, and I felt sorry for her.

"I'll bring the brown sugar to you," I said and touched her arm affectionately.

She squeezed my hand.

I went down the hill talking to myself: "Tiny Lambert, you are wonderful and beautiful. You are smart and popular and . . ."

# FOUR

When Vern came home shortly after five, it was obvious he had had something to drink. He was always in a good mood after two or three drinks, and loud and obnoxious after four or five. Then he would curl up somewhere and go to sleep. He didn't get mean like some men do. I knew kids who were whipped regular pretty hard. But Vern didn't hit us except for a rare swat on the butt. Sometimes he did get so mad you thought he was bound to kill somebody, but he got over it after storming and raging for a while. Or he just drove off in the pickup real fast and came back calm.

Vern was fifteen years older than Mama, and real short and stumpy. He put you in mind a whole lot of the movie comedian Lou Costello, except he wore denim britches and plaid shirts. He was getting a bald spot on the back of his head, and what hair was left was turning gray. His eyes were all the time bloodshot from too much bourbon, and the veins alongside his nose were broken. Vern's hands were rough and dirty from working in the mines. Even after he washed them good with lava soap, they were lined with coal dust in the wrinkles around his fingernails and knuckles.

That day he was in rare form. He was telling jokes and pinching Mama on the fanny. She was aggravated with him but she didn't let on. She hit at him playfully and bit her lip. We went out to get in the pickup to go to the store in Black Gap. I started to climb into the truck bed with the kids as usual when Vern said, "No, no, Tiny, you're in high school now. You ride up here in the cab with me and your mama."

A feather would have knocked me over I was so pleased. Mama smiled.

"Come on, honey," she said. "You can set in the middle."

I climbed in between them, grinning. Did this mean I was going to be treated like a grownup from now on? Vern backed the truck down the hill.

"Can you imagine what this child asked me for today, Vern?" Mama said.

"What in the world?" he said.

"Another pair of shoes!"

"Oh, Mama!" I protested. "Not just any shoes. Everybody at school had on white bucks today, Vern. Everybody but me. I just want to be like everybody else."

Vern didn't say a word.

Mama said something about everybody jumping off a cliff, but I wasn't listening. In about ten seconds flat she had ruined my ride in the cab.

"I'm going to the hardware," Vern announced when we were parked behind the A & P. "I'll be back in a minute."

Mama, the kids, and I went into the store. Every single time we went to the A & P, Phyllis started begging for something. It never failed, and you could hear her all over the store.

And Mama, every single time, would start up with, "Hush now, Phyllis. Be nice. Look at that pretty display. Hush now, Phyllis. Be nice."

Of course Phyllis would get worse, and it nearly drove me fruity. Then Luther would start in.

"Can I have a bottle of pop, Mama? Can I? Huh? Can I, Mama? Can I have a bottle of pop?"

Next Beau would whine for suckers. And all three of them were dirty and barefooted as usual.

I always lagged behind like I didn't know these people, and Mama would fuss at me, "Quit dawdling, Tiny!"

Dawdling? I'll declare she made that word up.

But that day Beau dawdled with me and he didn't say anything. I guess he was growing up because you could tell he was embarrassed, too.

When Phyllis began her high-pitched squeal, I knew there was no shutting her up, so I headed for the door, hoping I wouldn't see anybody I knew. I climbed in the truck and started to fantasize about Mr. Gillespie.

We are at a ball game and he offers me a ride home.

My hair is long and blond and shiny. I am wearing a pink evening dress with yards and yards of chiffon because I am the homecoming queen. Mr. Gillespie notices I am shivering.

"Here, take my coat," he says to me . . .

Vern climbed in the truck and tossed a shoe box my way. The lid was off that box so fast, and yes it was! Vern had gone and bought me some white bucks.

I squealed almost like Phyllis, and Vern grinned. Now, I am not a kissy person, never have been. It was years since I kissed anybody; and then it was Mama, and the kids when they were babies. But at that moment I threw my arms around Vern before I realized what it was I was going to do. Everything happened fast and I'm not sure how it came about, but what I meant to be a kiss on the cheek turned into something else. He squeezed me till I couldn't breathe, then stuck his tongue in my mouth and wiggled it around. I about gagged because his old tongue tasted sticky and rank with tobacco and bourbon.

I struggled and he let me go.

"Ugh!" I said, rubbing my mouth hard against the back of my hand. I wanted to spit, but I didn't want to insult him that bad. "Vern, what'd you do that for?"

Vern laughed a funny laugh, and he looked around at everything else but me.

"Well, try 'em on!" he finally said real loud. "I'll take 'em back right now if they don't fit."

I put on the shoes. Perfect fit, and beautiful! I could picture me wearing them in band tomorrow. Mr. Gillespie would see me.

"Well, I gotta go and pay the grocery bill," Vern said and left.

I placed the saddle oxfords inside the box and wore the white bucks. Then I spit out the door of the truck a few times, and wiped out the inside of my mouth with my dress tail, but I could still taste Vern's spit.

Ooooo . . . what got into him anyway?

# FIVE

⚰ "Tiny Lambert!" Bobby Lynn hollered my name all the way down the hall the next morning, and I was secretly pleased because just about everybody heard her. I waited for her to wade through the crowd to me.

"Hey, girl," she said. "Come on out and let's sit on the fence with Rosemary till homeroom."

"Who?"

"Rosemary Layne. You know her. She plays clarinet, too, and she sat on the other side of you yesterday in band."

"Oh," I said, but I didn't remember anybody in band except Bobby Lynn and Mr. Gillespie.

Bobby Lynn was wearing a summer dress and sandals, because it was still as warm as summer, and I learned that day that even though her mama worked at the Black Gap Style Shoppe, she didn't give a squeak who wore what when.

"Hey, Bobby Lynn," everybody called as we walked down the hall together. You could measure a person's popularity by the number of heys she got, because the morning hey was designed to pay homage. It seemed everybody knew and liked Bobby Lynn, and she was with me! We went out to the front campus, where I met Rosemary Layne. She was tall and dark, in contrast to me and Bobby Lynn. She had very large gray eyes and the longest, thickest lashes I ever saw. She was slender and elegant in a simple blue sheath. She was also warm and friendly.

"Hey, Tiny," she said sweetly, smiling. "Sit here by me."

I was surprised she knew my name. In fact I was surprised at nearly everything that morning. Somebody had actually hey'd me in the hall, and now somebody else was inviting me to sit with her. It seemed Tiny Lambert, who never had a real friend in her life, suddenly had friends coming after her! Did I have a sign on my back—PLEASE LOVE ME—or something?

Oh, well, I thought, as I perched on the rail fence between Bobby Lynn and Rosemary, they won't like me when they get to know me. Nobody ever does. But Aunt Evie's story about Lila's beautiful baby flashed through my mind. Maybe I would give it a chance. "I am a very nice person," I said to myself emphatically.

What followed was the Black Gap High School morning ritual. It went like this: first you perched on the fence for a while and watched other people strolling by. Then you strolled by the others while they perched and watched you. Sometimes you stopped to chat while you were strolling. The boys stayed perched in clusters here and there, but they could stroll, too, if they wanted.

Strolling and perching went on for a while, then all too soon the bell rang and it was time for homeroom. Bobby Lynn and Rosemary were in two of my other classes—English and history. I hadn't even noticed them the day before. Sixth period, I went flying up the stairs with my clarinet knocking against my knees. I opened the door to the band room, and there he was!

Mr. Gillespie looked right at me and said, "Hello."

I swallowed hard.

The music he handed out was "The Thunderer," and he walked in front of me, close enough that I could have reached out and touched one of his arms if I had wanted real bad to make a fool of myself.

Playing with the high school band for the first time thrilled me right down to my toes. There was a rich vibrant energy that I had never felt when I played with the beginners' band. Bobby Lynn and Rosemary felt it, too, and we played from the heart. Mr. Gillespie grinned like a pleased pup.

"I'll have to say it," he said when we finished "The Thunderer." "That was wonderful. I never expected you to be so good."

Even the seasoned upperclassmen bubbled over with pride and joy.

"He didn't know hillbillies could play like that," Jimmy Ted O'Quinn, always the clown, bellowed.

We all laughed. It was a special moment.

"Well, I must be in hillbilly heaven!" Mr. Gillespie responded. "Again! From the top!"

And he raised those arms.

Bobby Lynn, Rosemary, and I played the third and fourth clarinet parts while the upperclassmen played first and second. I decided I was going to be the best clarinet player Mr. Gillespie had ever heard. I planned to practice an hour a day, and two hours a day on weekends. My goal was to move up to first chair in one year.

I got my band uniform after school and carried it home on the bus. It was royal blue with a gold stripe up the leg and gold braids on the shoulders. Everybody on the bus had to admire and touch it, and at home the kids couldn't keep their grimy hands to themselves. So I hid my uniform way back in the closet.

I went outside to see Nessie, and she was waiting for me with her long bushy tail swishing, and her beautiful face pushed against the wire fence. I sat and told her all about my day at school. She was a good listener.

It was after six when Vern came home in his loud and obnoxious stage. He yelled up the stairs for Mama to come down; he had something to tell her. Beau, Luther, Phyllis, and I gathered around the kitchen table, silent and expectant. Mama appeared in her ratty housecoat, her brown hair standing straight up and her eyes all puffy from sleep. She looked awful.

"It's Maw," Vern said. "She's real bad off, and she wants to see the young'uns."

"Oh," Mama said.

"So git your clothes on!" Vern yelled. "And let's go."

"Can't she wait till tomorrow?"

That was a silly question and everybody knew it. When Vern's mama wanted something, she wanted it right now. She was always threatening to die on us, and she almost did die during the summer. We couldn't afford to take her threats lightly.

"Just get dressed, and shut up!" Vern said.

Mama was aggravated. I could tell she would rather be skinned alive than go see Maw Mullins, but she said nothing. She went up to her bedroom.

Vern turned to me.

"Tiny, you stay here and fix supper."

I knew that was coming. Maw Mullins never wanted me near her. I had four counts against me: (1) I was illegitimate; (2) I was female; (3) I was a Lambert; and (4) I had none of her blood in me. I was useless. But I didn't care. I never did like Maw Mullins, and I felt sorry for Beau and Luther the way she drooled over them. They didn't like her either. She didn't have much use for Phyllis because she was not a boy.

Mama came back in an almost clean dress, and her hair was plastered down.

"Just fry some taters, Tiny, and heat up the ham," she said to me. "There's corn bread in the Frigidaire."

Mama was always putting things in the refrigerator to keep the bugs out of them.

"We'll be back directly," she said.

The kids didn't even pretend to wash their faces or comb their hair, and nobody seemed to notice. They were barefooted, too, and it was getting nippy outside, but nobody noticed that either. They all piled in the pickup, ready to drive to Loggy Bottom, about sixteen miles up the river. I stood in the doorway trying to look solemn until they were out of sight. I was glad to be rid of them.

I took my clarinet into the kitchen and started my hour of practice. I squeaked a lot because my reed was bad, and I got tired of practicing real quick. After only twenty minutes I was making excuses for not practicing anymore, and I quit.

I went out on the porch and sat in the swing. The light was leaving the holler fast, but I could still see the road winding between the hills up toward Ruby Mountain.

Our neighbors were having supper. I could smell cabbage and pork, and somebody was frying onions. I could hear Cecil laughing, and his little sisters were squealing. I could hear spoons clanging against dishes.

Suddenly I thought about how much my life had changed in just two days. I was in love with Mr. Gillespie and I was a member of the high school band with a uniform and everything. I had two friends, and two pairs of school shoes, and we were getting a telephone.

This is nice, too, I thought, just sitting here in the twilight by myself and listening and smelling good smells.

I began to sing:

*Come home, come home, it's supper time,*
*The shadows lengthen fast.*

*Come home, come home, it's supper time,*
*We're going home at last.*

I sang about ten more songs, enjoying myself immensely. After a while I went in to fix supper, still singing. I peeled and fried the potatoes and set the ham and corn bread in the oven, but I wouldn't turn on the heat until everybody came home. I decided to open a can of peaches for dessert. Then all I could do was wait. I sat down at the kitchen table, propped my history book in front of me, and started studying. But I couldn't keep Mr. Gillespie out of my head.

We are coming up the holler in Mr. Gillespie's car —a red Chevy convertible. His coat is all wrapped around me and it smells like Old Spice. Suddenly, bam! Blowout. I am thrown against him. We can travel no farther.

"Oh, my dear," he says to me. "Forgive me for placing you in this trying predicament."

I turn to him slowly and the moonlight . . .

My face settled onto my history book as I drifted away.

# S I X

❧ I woke up with a start, my face numb. I sensed the lateness of the hour. Vern was standing in the kitchen doorway perfectly still, his face ashen.

"What is it?" I mumbled in confusion.

"She died," he said.

"Who? What! Maw Mullins is dead?"

"She died at 9:34 p.m. Eastern Standard Time," he said.

I never knew I could feel sorry for Vern. It was a brand-new sensation. He looked like a big kid standing there and I think he wanted to cry, but he didn't remember how. I got up and walked over to him.

"I'm awful sorry, Vern," I said, my voice cracking.

"Yeah, well . . ."

He just stood there, looking forlorn.

"Where's Mama?" I asked.

"Paw asked her to stay and take care of the arrangements. And the young'uns went to sleep."

"Well, are you hungry?"

"No, just put everything away, Tiny. I'm going to have a drink."

Vern moved to the cabinet and took out a bottle of bourbon. He poured a jelly glass half-full and filled it up the rest of the way with water. Then he took his drink, walked out on the front porch, and sat down in the swing.

I set the potatoes and ham and peaches in the refrigerator and went upstairs. I put on my pajamas, then pulled down the windows because the night air was chilly. I was tired and fell asleep without even thinking again of Mr. Gillespie or of Maw Mullins.

I don't know how long I slept when suddenly I came awake with a start. Something had jolted me, but I wasn't sure what. Next I was aware of a smell—bourbon. I turned my head slowly, and there was Vern sitting on the side of my bed.

"Don't be scared," he said in a hoarse whisper.

"What d'you want?" I said.

"I just want to touch you."

I scooted backward to the other side of the bed.

"You better go on now, Vern," I said, trying to sound calm.

He put out a hand toward me and I slipped to the floor opposite him. We looked at each other in the darkness. He was wheezing.

"Come on, Tiny," Vern finally said, and started

crawling drunkenly across my bed toward me. "I'm not going to hurt you."

I flew around the end of the bed and out of the room. Vern had no reflexes left at all. I was down the stairs when I heard him call my name.

I groped my way through the living room in the dark and crawled behind the couch. Only then did I realize I was shaking all over. I hunkered down and hugged my knees against my chest.

"Tiny!"

He was at the top of the stairs. I held my breath. I heard nothing for a long time, and I imagined him standing in the dark listening. I began to breathe again very softly, my heart flying. Then I heard uneven footsteps going down the hall. Maybe he was going to bed. I sat there on the hard floor until my behind was numb and I had to move. I crawled out slowly, not making a sound. Then I crept up the stairs, and to my relief I could hear Vern snoring from his bedroom.

I tiptoed to my room, closed my door, propped a chair under the doorknob, and crawled under the covers, shivering. I slept only in bits and pieces the rest of the night, and dreamed of Willa. I woke up early thinking of her for the first time in a very long time.

I decided to go to school as usual, even though Mama would wonder what in the world I was thinking of to go to school at such a time. She would want me at home to help out. But I didn't want to be alone with Vern, not ever again. And if I stayed, I would have to be alone with him until he went back up to Loggy Bottom. It didn't matter if Mama got mad at me, I was going to school. And I knew I could never tell Mama what happened. It would kill her.

I washed, dressed, and combed my hair. I thought my face looked paler and plainer than usual. I went quietly down the stairs with my books and my clarinet. The house seemed cold and cluttered and very, very lonely. Then I slipped out the door.

I was the first one at the bus stop, and Cecil was surprised to see me when he came out.

"Hey, Tiny, you're awful early."

I didn't say anything. I glanced up at my house to see if Vern was about, but the old house just hung there silently on the hill. It looked ugly. Suddenly, I hated it and I hated Vern.

"What's the matter, Tiny?" Cecil said gently.

Our eyes met, and for a split second I had the feeling he knew everything that had happened. My face went hot. I turned my back to him and looked toward Ruby Mountain.

"Nothing" was all I said.

In band that day Mr. Gillespie had on short sleeves again, and when I looked at his arms I felt this great rush of shame. I felt guilty of something, but I had done nothing wrong. And I was oh, so sad. I wanted to go back to last week, to yesterday, before this hateful, hurtful thing robbed me of . . . of what? I didn't know what, but something was gone from me. I wanted to be alone—to cry—to curl up with Willa and go back to being a little girl, and never grow up.

When the bus dropped me off at home I walked

slowly up the hill. The pickup was parked under the porch, which meant Vern was there. I wondered if he was alone.

I dawdled.

I stopped to see Nessie. Maybe I would go to Aunt Evie's.

"Boy, Mama's mad at you," I heard Phyllis say as she came up beside me.

I was relieved, but I didn't speak to her. Phyllis followed me into the house. The boys were at the kitchen table and Vern and Mama were upstairs.

"What's going on tonight?" I said to them.

"We're going back to Paw's," Beau said. "How come you went to school when you didn't have to?"

I didn't answer.

There was a peck basket full of apples on the floor, and I took one. I knew they came from Maw and Paw's place. They always had the best apples.

"Mama's mad at you," Phyllis repeated.

I still ignored her.

I sat down by Beau and bit into my apple.

"Tell me about last night," I said to him.

"Tell you what? She died, that's all," Beau said.

"Was the doctor there?"

"No. You can die without a doctor, you know."

He and Luther giggled.

"Well, did you see her die?"

"Nope. Just Daddy and Paw and Aunt Tootsie were in the room with her."

"Did you see her after she died?"

"Yeah."

"How'd she look?"

"Dead."

The boys giggled again.

"Be serious, Beau Mullins!"

"I am serious!" he said. "She looked dead and she *was* dead! Ain't that serious?"

"It was the same as when she was alive," Luther volunteered. "Only she didn't talk. I never saw her quiet before."

We sat still for a moment, then exploded with laughter.

"Sh . . . sh . . ." I tried to shush them as I pointed to Mama and Vern's bedroom.

We heard footsteps on the stairs, and all the merriment left my heart. I knew it was Vern. He came into the room, and I went on eating my apple without glancing at him.

"You can stay home tonight, Tiny," he said. "If you want to."

That was a surprise.

"Me too," Phyllis said. "I don't want to go to no wake."

"Me neither," Beau and Luther said together.

"No," Vern said. "The rest of us have to go. But Maw didn't treat Tiny right."

That was a bigger surprise. I never thought Vern noticed.

"Well, anyway, Mama's mad at Tiny," Phyllis said for the third time, but this time everybody ignored her.

Vern spent most of his time with Paw Mullins the week after the funeral, so Mama played sick and stayed in bed. She wouldn't get up for nothing or nobody, and I started thinking I didn't like her. The kids went to school dirty and ran around the holler like a pack of wild dogs.

One chilly night I made bacon, eggs, and gravy for supper, and it was good, but I couldn't cook much else, so we ate a lot of bologna. When Vern was home, I wouldn't look at him, and I didn't speak to him at all. He didn't speak to me either without he had to. Mostly I stayed in my room when I wasn't in school.

The big day for the telephone installation came. Mama got up to show where to run the line by the staircase in the hall downstairs, and the telephone man lectured us on telephone courtesy and proper usage.

When he left, we stood looking at each other and the black object, grinning. We each listened to the dial tone, and hung up the receiver. I decided to wait until the hall was clear to call Bobby Lynn and Rosemary and give them my number, which was 4054.

Our first call came while we were standing there admiring the telephone. It was four short rings, and Mama picked it up.

"Hello, this is the Vernon Mullins residence," she said.

It was the telephone company checking out the line. When Mama hung up, we heard the rings for the other parties on our line—one long ring or three short rings or a combination of long and short rings.

Ruby Valley had joined hands with the rest of the U.S.A.

# SEVEN

⚹ Aunt Evie asked me if I would help her put up apple butter on Saturday. The Hesses were supplying the apples, jars, sugar, and spices and a generous supply of apple butter for Aunt Evie if she would do all the work. Working with Aunt Evie was fun because she always told jokes and stories and kept me entertained, so I said yes.

No sooner was that settled when Bobby Lynn called me and said, "Let's you and me and Rosemary go see *I'd Climb the Highest Mountain* next Saturday. It's got William Lundigan and Susan Hayward."

Gosh, I wanted to go with her, but how could I let Aunt Evie down?

So I told Bobby Lynn all about Aunt Evie, how

everybody loved her and gave her stuff, that she got jilted, and she listened to your problems.

"Well, maybe I'd like to put up apple butter, too," Bobby Lynn said, which like to have surprised me to pieces. "Did you ever think of that, huh?"

"You mean it, Bobby Lynn?"

"Yeah."

"Do you think Rosemary will come, too?" I asked.

"I'll call her and see."

At first I felt uneasy about Aunt Evie, so when I got off the phone I went up the hill to see what she thought of strangers invading her premises. I should have known it! Aunt Evie was tickled to death and she danced a jig right there in her kitchen.

"Hit's just like when I was a girl! We did things like that all the time. We'll build a big fire outside, and . . ."

She was off and running, laying plans for Saturday. The rest of the week we gathered wood and got together all the things we needed. She had a big black pot to cook the apples in, and from several kitchens we collected bowls and knives for peeling and slicing, and buckets for peels and cores.

Mr. Hess and Cecil brought the apples in baskets and put them in Aunt Evie's back yard. I helped carry the jars, and Cecil's little brothers and sisters pitched in and delivered the sugar and spices.

Saturday morning I woke up with this tune going around in my head:

> *There once lived an Indian maid,*
> *A shy little prairie maid,*

*Who sang a lay, a love song gay,*
*As on the plain she'd while away the day.*

It was nerves. Every time I got nervous, some silly ditty started up in my head, and no matter what I did, it wouldn't shut up.

What if Bobby Lynn and Rosemary were bored? What if they thought I was stupid and Aunt Evie was stupid and we lived in a stupid place on a stupid hill, and canning apple butter was a stupid thing to do on a Saturday?

*She loved a warrior bold, this shy little maid of old,*
*But brave and gay, he rode one day to battle far away.*

But one thing I did know and that was what to wear this time. Both Bobby Lynn and Rosemary said they were wearing their blue jeans and their daddy's white shirts. I stole Vern's only white shirt, and I didn't care if he got mad at me. It was worth it. And from Rosemary's daddy's general store, for only sixty-nine cents each, Rosemary had bought us dog collars, which were the absolute rage at school. They were plastic, and you wore them around the top of your bobby socks on one ankle. Mine was yellow, Rosemary's was red, and Bobby Lynn's was green. I had rolled my hair tight, and when I brushed it out around my face, it looked all right.

The world outside was crisp and clear, the changing hills brilliant against a perfectly blue sky.

Bobby Lynn and Rosemary arrived about ten-thirty. Rosemary's brother, Hassell, brought them in their daddy's black Ford pickup. Hassell was sixteen and tall, with gray eyes like Rosemary's and a shock of black hair almost hanging down into his eyes. He made me nervous, and my heart was flying, my mind racing. I was surprised when Hassell offered to carry the Cokes and Nabs that they had brought from their daddy's store up to Aunt Evie's. I steered the three of them quickly around my house, scared one of them might want to go in there. I knew Mama and Vern were still in bed, and the house and young'uns were a big mess as always.

Aunt Evie met us at her door as excited as a girl.

"You're Rosemary," she said. "Tiny told me you were tall and pretty. And here's Bobby Lynn, looking like a doll. Tell me, Bobby Lynn, is Clint Clevinger your grandpa?"

"Why, he sure is. You know him?"

"I useter. Yeah, I useter. Don't no more. And who is this handsome feller?"

"This is my brother, Hassell," Rosemary said.

Then who do you think came up the hill at that very moment? Why, Cecil Hess!

"Hey," he said cheerfully. "Hassell, I saw you, and I said to myself, 'I bet me and old Hassell can get this show on the road.'"

Hassell grinned. Bobby Lynn giggled. She thought Cecil was the stuff. Then here came Beau, Luther, and Phyllis. I about died.

"Now, y'all just go on back home!" I stomped my foot at them. "Nobody invited you."

Rosemary put her arm around Phyllis.

"Ain't she cute?" she said.

Well, I'll tell you one thing, she wouldn't think she was so cute if she could hear her squealing in the A & P. But Phyllis had herself a hero on the spot. Beau and Luther latched on to Hassell like leeches, and nobody seemed to mind but me. Then Cecil's brothers and sisters arrived one at a time. I was ready to chew off my fingernails. Directly, J. C. Combs, Joyce Boyd, and Dolly Horn came, and we all busted out laughing. It was a full-fledged party, and I was no longer in charge of anything. I could relax.

Pretty soon young folks packed Aunt Evie's yard and spilled over into the woods. We were all peeling apples, laughing, and joking, while Aunt Evie flitted about, happy as a jaybird, hollering instructions.

The black pot sat over the fire right in the middle of the yard, and when she started adding the spices to those bubbling apples, the aroma was enough to make you foam at the mouth. We dipped out a bowl full of half-done apple butter and passed it around for everybody to sample on a piece of bread. It was good, and it whet our appetites for other refreshments.

Somehow we accumulated hot dogs, candy bars, potato chips, pickles, suckers, and bubble gum, and I don't know what all else. It seemed every time we finished off one thing, something else appeared in its place. Cecil, J.C., and Hassell were running back and forth to the coal company store down the creek, and then the adults started coming with more food.

The Horns and the Hesses came first with a big cake and fresh apple cider. They helped us finish the apple butter, and we wound up with fifty-four quarts all in a row on Aunt Evie's front porch.

Then the Combs family and Mama and Vern came with sandwiches and Kool-Aid. Mama was cleaned up, and she looked nice.

"This is my mother," I introduced her to Bobby Lynn and Rosemary, and they said hey.

Vern just stood there expecting me to introduce him, too.

"And this is Vern," I said quickly.

He was looking at me in his only white shirt that swallowed me whole. I turned my back to him and bounced away. He said hello to my friends, then wandered over to talk to Mr. Horn. I guess they talked about guns all afternoon. What can you say about a gun after a minute? They make a loud noise. What else can you say? They kill things. And not much else. Anyway, Vern had this ugly musket hanging on the wall in the living room right over that hole that used to be the fireplace. For a long time, Mr. Horn had coveted that gun to add to his collection. He had a whole bunch of guns, some of them rusty, some of them centuries old. He had used every trick in the book to get that gun from Vern, and nothing worked.

I noticed Hassell was following Dolly Horn around and she wasn't paying any attention to him. She liked a boy from Princeton, West Virginia, who she met at 4-H camp. Cecil and Bobby Lynn seemed to be hitting it off. I thought of Mr. Gillespie and wished with all my heart he was here, too. But putting up apple butter was probably the last thing in the world you would ever see him doing.

By suppertime the air had grown cool and Bobby Lynn, Rosemary, and I sat near the fire with Aunt

Evie. We each had a wad of green bubble gum to work on, but mine was the biggest. Then Aunt Evie started telling us about Ward.

"I lived up Glory Holler back then on the side of a hill kinda like here," she said. "And Ward lived down toward Harry's Branch. When he came to court me, he yodeled for me down the road, and you could hear him coming from a long ways off. When I'd hear him a-yodeling, I'd yodel back to him."

"Can you yodel, Aunt Evie?" Rosemary and Bobby Lynn said together.

"Course I can yodel!"

"Oh, do it! Do it!" Bobby Lynn squealed. "I just love yodeling!"

And bless Pat if Aunt Evie didn't stand up right there by the fire in the cool of the evening and yodel her head off! It sent chills right up my spine because I never did hear anybody yodel any better, not even Carolina Cotton in the movies.

People stopped whatever it was they were doing and looked at Aunt Evie and listened to her yodeling.

Now, you might not believe this, but I saw forty-six years fall off that old woman. I saw a young girl standing there yodeling to her beau, and I think others shared the same vision.

When she was finished, nobody moved or spoke because the echo was still bouncing off the hills. Then we applauded and cheered.

Bobby Lynn was speechless. She really did love yodeling, and I think she decided right then that Aunt Evie was going to teach her to yodel.

"I never heard the beat," Rosemary said.

Aunt Evie just shrugged.

"Everybody nearabouts yodeled when I was a girl. Hit was a signal to say, 'Here I come.' Nowadays you just toot your old car horn. Ain't near as pretty."

As darkness came, we grew quiet, and started cleaning up. Bobby Lynn and Rosemary were the first to take their leave along with Hassell. I hated like the devil to see them go.

"Aunt Evie," Bobby Lynn said, "I don't know when I've had a better time."

"Me too," Rosemary agreed.

"Me three," chorused the others.

"Well, you can thank Tiny," Aunt Evie said and put an arm around me. "Hit was her doing."

I was embarrassed, and I bent over and fiddled around with my dog collar.

That night I was so wound up I felt like I would never sleep again. Beside me Phyllis was out cold as I lay looking out at the moon over the hills.

*Now, the moon shines tonight on pretty Red Wing,*
*The breeze is sighing, the night bird's crying . . .*

# EIGHT

⊁ In the weeks following, autumn exploded and so did my social life.

Splatters of orange and red . . . the aroma of burning leaves and sharp winds crackling down the holler . . . the shrill new sound of the telephone ringing!

"It's for Tiny . . . again!"

Football season, first downs and touchdowns . . . perfect skies and a flurry of blue and gold ever whichaway you looked . . . "The Star-Spangled Banner" . . . cold, clear nights and school spirit.

*Hail, Black Gap High School,*
*Three cheers for our dear alma mater!*

Pounding drums and parades . . . left—right . . . chills and cheers.

*Strawberry shortcake, huckleberry pie!*
*V – I – C – T – O – R – Y.*
*Will we win it?*
*You doggone right!*
*Black Gap High School,*
*Fight! Fight! Fight!*

Boys, winks and giggles, hot chocolate and Sousa marches . . . our rivals—Bluefield and Richlands and Big Lick—tucked away in the little dips and grooves of the hills like lurking beasts . . . my first best friends, Bobby Lynn and Rosemary, and Mr. Gillespie, of course, presiding over all, laughing and cheering with us, waving his baton, flitting in and out of my dreams, both waking and sleeping.

It was truly a magic season, but as suddenly as it had begun, it ended. The last football game was played at Black Gap. Afterward, as the crowd milled around, and the parking lot turned into a traffic jam, Rosemary, Bobby Lynn, and I slipped away to a quiet spot on the front campus. In our band uniforms we lay on our backs, looking up at the white steeple of the school against the sky. We were so close by then nothing needed to be said.

Suddenly our thoughts were interrupted by a frightening male voice.

"What's yer name, girl?"

The three of us jumped to our feet gasping as a man stepped out of the shadows. We faced the intruder.

He was old and stooped over, using a walking stick. He had a long, white beard, and was wearing a toboggan cap over his ears, a red plaid jacket, and overalls.

We were speechless.

"Speak up! What's yer name?" he repeated, and he poked me so hard in the shoulder with his stick I about fell backward, but Bobby Lynn and Rosemary caught me.

"Ti—Tiny Lambert," I stammered.

"*Huh!*" he snorted loudly, and spit a big splat of tobacco juice on the grass. "You live up Ruby Valley with them Mullinses?"

I nodded.

Rosemary edged away from me. She was about to run for help.

"What? Can't hear your head shaking, girl!" he hollered.

"Yes!" I spoke up. "I live up Ruby Valley with my mother, Hazel Mullins, and my stepfather, Vernon Mullins. Who are you?"

"None of yer goddamn business!"

That made me mad, and we stood glaring at each other for a minute. Then he turned abruptly and left us standing there.

"Who do you reckon . . . ?"

"I don't know," I said quickly, shivering. "Let's get back to the others."

Late that night the face of the old man came back to haunt me. Oh, I knew him all right, though I was surprised I could remember. It was a face from the misty past—a face I associated with Willa, and running

across a windy mountaintop, and the taste of strawberries. Grandpa Lambert.

Bobby Lynn started spending every Saturday with
Aunt Evie learning how to yodel. On pretty days I
could hear them up there practicing outside. At lunch
I joined them and we gossiped and giggled as we ate
something good that Bobby Lynn had brought from
her house.

Rosemary's birthday was on a Saturday in February
and she invited me and Bobby Lynn to come to her
house and spend the day and night with her. She lived
about twelve miles outside of Black Gap. Then a big
snow came on that very day, but Bobby Lynn's daddy
put chains on his tires and took us anyway.

It was fun driving through the snow and seeing how
pretty everything was. We were in high spirits as we
climbed out of Mr. Clevinger's car and went into Rosemary's daddy's store.

Rosemary was helping out, but when we went in,
her daddy excused her. She bundled up and we went
out the back door of the store right on the river. Before
us was a swinging bridge suspended all the way across
the river—about thirty or forty yards to the opposite
bank where the railroad tracks were. Beyond the
tracks, nestled against the hillside, was the Laynes'
cozy white house with smoke coming from the
chimney.

"You live over there?" I cried out in amazement.
"We have to go over that bridge?"

"Sure," Rosemary said. "Come on, I'll show you how
to walk it. It's fun."

Rosemary struck off across the bridge. It was about three feet wide, with a high mesh-wire fence and a cable on each side so there was no danger of falling off.

It was obvious Rosemary was an expert at navigating that bridge. It began to sway—like a bed does when you walk on it. She grabbed a cable and grinned at me and Bobby Lynn from the center.

"Come on! You have to pick up the rhythm of the bridge."

So we took off after her, laughing. But that bridge was a trick you didn't learn just by watching somebody else. Every time you thought it was going to swing to the right, it went left. And every time you thought it was going to dip, it rose up at you instead. After about ten steps, Bobby Lynn and I had the silly giggles so bad we just stood there hanging on to each other, and to the cable. Rosemary had to come and get us. A few steps at a time, she guided us across the river and up onto the railroad tracks on the other side.

Rosemary's house was comfortable and clean. They had a big fire going in a fireplace in the living room, and in front of it was a huge round thick rug. I could smell some good sweet thing baking—probably a birthday cake. A television set was turned on in the corner of the room.

Hassell came out of the kitchen with a glass of milk and an enormous sandwich in his hands, and his mouth was pooched out and running over.

"Hi, Hassell!" we said, and he waved his full hands around, while trying to do justice to the load in his mouth.

We laughed. We were prone to laugh at anything.

Mrs. Layne came in from the kitchen wiping her hands on her apron. She was a warm, friendly woman who looked like a middle-aged version of Rosemary.

"Come in, girls. Take off your coats. Ain't it awful out there?"

"No, no, we're going to build a snowman," Rosemary said. "I just came in to ask you to make us some hot tea to drink with the cake."

"Fine, fine," Mrs. Layne said.

We went back outside.

"I want to go on the bridge again," Bobby Lynn said when the snowman was almost finished.

"Me too!" I said.

"Sure we will," Rosemary said.

The bridge probably was not that much fun for Rosemary, but she was always agreeable.

"After that we'll go in and have some cake and tea and watch television," Rosemary said.

"Yeah!"

We finished our snowman and went on the bridge. Back and forth we traipsed, lunged, swayed, giggling all the time until suddenly Bobby Lynn and I discovered the secret, picked up the rhythm, and waltzed across without missing a step.

We met in the middle, hung on to the cable for balance, and gazed out at the half-frozen river and the white hills. The sun was out by then, and we knew the snow wouldn't last long under its brilliance.

"Yodel for us, Bobby Lynn," I said.

"Oh, do!" Rosemary squealed.

"I'm not too good at it yet," she said.

"We don't care. Do it," I said.

"Okay," Bobby Lynn conceded. "Y'all sing 'When I Lived in the Valley,' and when you get to the yodeling part, I'll do it."

So we did.

> *When I lived in the valley,*
> *And my sweetheart in the hills,*
> *Our signal was*
> *Odel . . . odel . . . le . . . di . . . whoo!*

Off she went. She wasn't Aunt Evie, but her yodeling sounded pretty.

> *One day I went to call upon*
> *My pretty little miss,*
> *And I didn't hear her*
> *Odel . . . odel . . . le . . . di . . . whoo!*

Rosemary and I applauded for her. We were in the mood and we sang some more. We did "It Don't Hurt Anymore," "Oh Baby Mine," and "The Great Pretender." Then we started on "I'll See You in the Spring." I really loved that song, and let loose. I threw back my head and looked at the sky where the sun was dancing, and I was thinking what a wonderful day it was.

> *I'll see you in the willow*
> *Weeping in the stream.*
> *I'll see you in the newborn fawn*
> *Soft as in a dream.*

> *I'll stand high on a mountain*
> *And watch young birds take wing.*
> *And though you won't be there,*
> *I'll see you in the spring.*

That's when it occurred to me that I was singing all by myself. I clamped my mouth shut and jerked my head toward Bobby Lynn and Rosemary. They were just looking at me with these goofy, dumbfounded expressions. I felt the blood rush to my face. What kind of blunder had I made this time?

"What'sa matter?"

"What's the matter?" Bobby Lynn said incredulously as she put her hands on her hips. "Girl, I never knew you could sing like that!"

"Like what?"

"I never knew anybody could sing like that," Rosemary added with awe in her voice. "Except Patti Page or Teresa Brewer."

I was too stunned to speak.

"That was wonderful, Tiny," Bobby Lynn said.

They were serious. They really liked my singing.

"You know," Rosemary said, "they're doing a talent show this year."

"No, I didn't know," Bobby Lynn said. "When?"

"After the beauty contest. They're doing it so the boys will have something to compete in. But it's for everybody. Y'all have to be in it. Tiny can sing and you can yodel."

"Sing some more," Bobby Lynn said to me.

But I had a sudden attack of shyness.

"Not by myself. Y'all sing with me."

We started a lot of songs together, which I finished by myself. Afterward we went in and watched television. Mrs. Layne made sandwiches and popcorn, birthday cake and tea.

We watched *Judge Roy Bean, Fury*, and *Huntington Dance Party* before the evening news came on.

All the time my mind was racing giddily: "I can sing! I can sing!"

# NINE

⊁ Me and Mr. Gillespie are sitting in his car at the
drive-in movie at the mouth of Glory on a Saturday
night. We are both wearing short sleeves and our arms
touch . . .

"Play me some checkers." Luther plopped down
beside me in the porch swing, and jolted Mr. Gillespie
right out of my head. It was a beautiful Sunday in early
May, a few days after my fifteenth birthday. I was in
shorts for the first time of the season, and a bird was
singing from a treetop, "Pret-ty! Pret-ty!"

"Oh, Luther," I groaned. "Not now. It's not a checkers day."

Luther grinned. "Wouldn't you like to whup me
today?"

"Huh!"

That was a joke. Luther was the undisputed checkers champ of Ruby Valley—maybe the world. He could
beat anybody. Sometimes strangers showed up at the
door to challenge Luther, and they always went away
shaking their heads. Luther had just turned nine and
he'd been at it for three years. It was a freak thing
because he couldn't do anything else. He still couldn't
read, or add more than two numbers together. Sometimes he had trouble tying his shoestrings, but he sure
could play checkers.

"You ain't played me in a long time," he said.
"Maybe you can beat me now."

He grinned again, showing two big rabbit teeth in
front and a red tongue where he'd been licking dry
cherry Jell-O out of the package.

"Sure, Luther," I said. "And maybe President Ei-
senhower will come to supper tonight."

"Oh, come on, Tiny."

I looked at the hills, which were all filled out with
green again. Oh, what a perfect day, I thought, to
spend with someone wonderful like Mr. Gillespie . . .
to go romping in the wild places, holding hands.

"If you'll play me a game, I'll tell you something I
heard Cecil say about you."

"What? What'd he say? Cecil Hess? Huh! Was he
talking about me? I don't care what Cecil Hess said
about me. What was it?"

"Play me a game."

"I don't want to play checkers and I don't care what
Cecil Hess said about me. Was it good or bad?"

"I'll lay out the board," Luther said and pulled up

a crate he kept there on the porch for this very purpose. Then he sat down on the floor cross-legged and laid out the checkers. He always played black. I was red.

"Who did he say it to?"

"Your move."

"Was he talking to you?"

"No, he was talking to Roger Altizer on the telephone."

"Luther! Were you listening in on the party line?"

"No, I just picked it up and heard your name."

Luther made one of his brilliant moves.

"Why don't you just jump 'em all now and get it over with?" I said.

He laughed. He was in his glory.

"So what'd Cecil say about me?"

"He said somebody likes you."

"Somebody? Who?"

"I dunno. Some boy thinks you're cute and he likes you."

"Who? Who?"

"That's all I heard."

"You mean Cecil said, 'Somebody likes Tiny'? Just somebody?"

"No, he said the name."

"And?"

"And what? Tiny, you can't move there."

"His name, stupid, what's his name?"

"I don't remember."

"Luther, did you make all that up?"

"No, go ask Cecil."

"I can't do that."

He jumped my last two men, and the game was over.

"One more game," he said.

"No!"

"Why not? Didn't I tell you what Cecil said?"

"But you didn't get the name."

The telephone rang.

Inside the house I heard Beau and Phyllis go scrambling, and at the same time I made my own mad dash, stumbling over Luther on the way, and the checkers went flying.

Luther said a real bad word, and I yelled at him over my shoulder, "You had something in your mouth I wouldn't even have in my hand!"

Phyllis beat me to the phone.

"Hey, Dixie," she said. "Mama's still in bed. Daddy is, too. What d'you want?"

Dixie was Mama's childhood friend who I couldn't stand. She was always asking me personal questions like, "What size bra you into now, Tiny?"

"Here, talk to Tiny," Phyllis said, and thrust the phone into my hands.

"Hey, Dixie," I said.

"Tiny, I need to talk to Hazel right now, so go git 'er."

"I can't do that, Dixie. She's asleep, and you know how she is when she's woke up."

"Well, Tiny Lambert, your Grandpa Lambert died last night. I just found out when I got to the hospital for my shift. You want to be the one to tell your mama?"

"Died? What of?"

"Meanness probably, but that's not for me to say. You want to break the news to Hazel?"

"No, I'll go get her."

"Well, make it snappy. I ain't got all day."

I went slow, rehearsing what I was going to say to Mama. I knocked on her door.

"Mama?"

No answer. I waited.

I knocked a second time.

"Mama?"

"Don't knock on that door again, Tiny!" she hollered.

"Mama, Dixie's on the phone, and she says it's real, real important."

"Dixie's hind end!" Vern snorted.

"Mama," I said. "It's an emergency."

I didn't hear anything for a long time.

"Mama," I called again, exasperated.

Being between Mama and Dixie was a hard place to be.

"All right. All right," Mama mumbled. "Tell 'er I'm coming."

So I went to the phone and told Dixie Mama was coming, then I went back out on the porch and sat in the swing.

"I can't find all my checkers!" Luther sputtered. "You gotta buy me some more!"

"Shh . . ." I tried to hush him. "I'll help you find them. Now listen . . ."

Mama could be heard on the stairs.

"What is it?" Luther whispered, and sat down by me.

"Just listen."

"Hey, Dixie," Mama said. "Something the matter?"

Silence for a minute.

Then, "Oh."

That's all she said.

"Grandpa Lambert died," I whispered to Luther.

"Mama's daddy?"

"Yeah."

"Thank you, Dixie," Mama said. "No, you don't need to come. I gotta think. 'Bye now."

And that was that. Mama went back to bed. Derndest thing.

I thought about the night I saw Grandpa Lambert at school. I never did tell Mama about that because I thought it would upset her. One time I heard her say she saw him in Black Gap and he wouldn't talk to her. She cried. But that was long ago. Maybe she didn't care anymore.

I sat swinging and thinking about Grandpa and Mama for a long time. It seemed like such a waste for them not to see each other all those years just because . . . because why? A stupid feud between the Mullinses and the Lamberts a hundred years ago.

About an hour later, Mama came downstairs wearing her britches, an old plaid shirt, and a straw hat. She came out and sat beside me and lit a cigarette.

"Did Dixie tell you what happened?" she said.

"Yeah."

"Tiny, let's you and me go up to Ruby Mountain."

"Okay."

"I got to decide what to do. The body's at Childress's Funeral Home, and I don't want to bring it here."

"Don't he have some more kin somewheres?"

"No, his family all moved down to Ohio back in the

thirties, 'cept for him. He lost track of them, and I don't even know their names. There was me and my mother and my brother, Danny James. But they both died of scarlet fever when I was fourteen. That left just me and Daddy till you came along two years later."

Vern came down the stairs and stood in the doorway with the screen door open.

"Well, come on," he said, and took the pickup key off its hook just inside the front door.

"Where you going to?" Phyllis called from inside the house. "I wanna go."

"No," Mama said. "Just me and Tiny. Get me a bucket out of the kitchen, Phyllis."

Phyllis came out and stood beside Vern.

"A bucket? What for?"

"The strawberries are ripe up on the mountain. Go on now."

"Cain't I go, Daddy?" Phyllis said sweetly and sidled up to him.

"She can ride along," Vern said to Mama. "We'll drop y'all off and come back for you later."

"I reckon," Mama conceded. "But get me that bucket, Phyllis. The blue chipped one with the daisies on it."

"I get to go, too, *Ha! Ha! Ha!*" Phyllis couldn't help needling me as she went in.

The rest of us went down the tall steps. I climbed in the back of the truck because I wasn't about to sit beside Vern in my shorts. Then Phyllis came out with the bucket and we backed down the hill onto the dirt road. We headed up the holler toward Ruby Mountain, and Phyllis started singing a silly song about a poor old woman who swallowed a fly, and my mind drifted away.

Mama was just a year older than me when she got pregnant with me.

Mama, I thought, what were you like? Did you have daydreams like mine? Did you love my daddy like I love Mr. Gillespie?

The truck began to climb up between two mountains that grew closer and closer together, and the road grew narrower and rockier. Pretty soon it was no more than a cow path with big rocks sticking out of the ground; then the road wound around the face of the mountain like a belt riding up, and you could look down over the side of the truck straight down into a holler far, far below. One slip of the wheel, and . . .

I visualized the truck bouncing down the mountain, turning over and over, spilling us out and squashing us.

It is stroll-and-perch time on Monday morning. Tiny Lambert is on everyone's lips.

"She was a wonderful person," they say. "Wonderful."

"Nobody knew just how wonderful she really was," Bobby Lynn says.

"She was never appreciated for her marvelous singing talent," Rosemary says.

And in band, Mr. Gillespie announces that Tiny Lambert is to be buried in the graveyard there on the hill outside the band-room window where she can always hear the music she loved so much . . .

"I don't want to pick strawberries anyhow," Phyllis was saying.

The road leveled out and we were riding across the top of the mountain. It was covered with daisies and violets and other blooming things. You could look out and see for miles—mountains and valleys, and the sky was all around us. You didn't have to look straight up to see it.

A memory flashed before my mind's eye: a memory of me and Willa, tumbling and laughing in the wild-flowers. And I felt like I was coming home.

# TEN

⚑ The truck stopped in front of a log cabin. Honest
to goodness, it looked like Abe Lincoln's birthplace or
something. Mama got out of the truck and stood there
staring at the house. I got out and stood beside her.

"I'll be back about four," Vern called.

Mama didn't say anything. Phyllis climbed out, set
the bucket on the porch, and climbed up front with
Vern.

"Okay?" Vern yelled. "Four o'clock?"

"Okay," Mama said, not taking her eyes from the
cabin.

Vern turned the truck around and left.

"It ain't changed a bit," Mama said.

I didn't say anything because I didn't remember the

cabin. Mama walked slowly around it, and I followed.

Suddenly a wonderful aroma floated over us . . . as sweet and delicate as . . . Willa! It was Willa's smell. Was she here? I turned around and around, expecting to see her.

"Honeysuckle," Mama said as she paused, threw back her head, closed her eyes, and breathed in deeply. "That aroma was thick in the air the day you were born, Tiny."

"Honeysuckle?" I said. "Where is it?"

"There." Mama pointed to a broken-down fence running at a distance. It was covered with green foliage and small peach-colored flowers. "It grows wild everywhere up here and blooms in May."

"It's beautiful," I said breathlessly. "Oh, Mama, it's all so beautiful. How could you leave this place?"

Mama laughed and put her arm around me.

"It was a prison to me," she said. "Beautiful, yes, but still a prison. I thought life was something that was happening to someone else, somewhere else."

We walked together. Then there it was: the greenest, flowingest, most beautiful weeping willow tree in the world. Anyone who has never seen a weeping willow is deprived. It grows like an umbrella, its slender pendent branches filled out with tiny leaves sweeping the ground in places, as it weeps, sweeps, sways.

"Do you remember playing under there?" Mama asked.

"No, but oh, Mama, I love it!"

"You always did. In one way I hated to take you away from all this."

"Oh, I wish you hadn't!"

Mama sighed. "I felt life was passing me by."

"But why Vern, Mama?"

"Just to get away," Mama admitted. "Don't you see? I was suffocating. I would have married anybody who would take me away."

"And was life with Vern any better?"

Mama got tears in her eyes, and I felt this great rush of pity. I hugged her real tight; then we just stood there holding each other and crying. I was crying because she was crying, and I wasn't quite sure why she was crying.

"Oh, Tiny, I was so young I didn't know what to do."

"I know, Mama."

"And I wanted a better life for both of us. Vern seemed a way out."

"I know. I know."

"It is twelve miles from here to Black Gap," Mama said. "And we had no car. I couldn't go to the store when I wanted, or see a movie, or meet other young people. I couldn't even go to church."

We crawled up under the weeping willow then, and sat on the ground. It was a cool, private, dark world where you could barely see out, and nobody could see in. All around us the branches swept toward the ground, touching it gently in places.

"And Vern's been good to me, Tiny. Ain't he been good to you?"

I didn't say anything.

"Now, Tiny, you needn't sit there and tell me Vern ain't been good to you."

"I reckon," I said.

"You reckon what?"

"He's been good to me for the most part."

"All of us," Mama said. "I don't know how we would survive without him."

"But did you never love Vern, Mama?"

Mama took a deep breath.

"That's right, Tiny. I never did."

That seemed like the saddest thing of all, for two people to live together all these years and have three children together while one of them was lonely in her heart.

"Vern's okay," I said. "When he's not drinking."

I leaned back onto the cool ground, breathed in the smell of honeysuckle, and looked up at the branches of the tree. This must have been where Willa got her name. Every day of my babyhood, I probably heard the phrase "pretty willow."

"What was my daddy like?" I said quickly, then held my breath. I never dreamed I would ask Mama that question.

"He was just a boy," Mama said softly. "Just seventeen."

"Do I look like him?"

"No, you look like me, Tiny. He had bright red curly hair and freckles and green eyes."

"Red hair!"

"Yeah, the reddest, curliest mop I ever did see."

"Did you love him lots?"

"Yes, I still do. But I guess he died in the war. His own mama never heard from him again, and the army to this day can't say what happened to him."

"What was his name?"

"Ernest Bevins. He was from Shortt's Gap."

Ernest Bevins! And he had curly red hair like Willa's. What a strange, strange thing!

"Wanna go pick some strawberries, Tiny?"

"Sure."

We crawled out and I followed Mama a ways across the mountaintop behind the cabin. We came upon a spring of sparkling clear water bubbling up out of the ground.

"This is where we got all our water," Mama said and knelt down by the spring. She took water in her hands and drank it.

"Ahh . . . still the best water in the world."

I drank some, and it really was good—much better than what we had down in the holler. Our water was full of iron. It tasted bad and smelled bad, and stained the sinks and tub and toilet a rusty red color. You couldn't scrub it off to save your hide.

Beyond the spring was a huge strawberry patch. It went a long ways back and spread down over the side of the mountain. I never saw so many strawberries, and they were ruby-red ripe.

"Mama," I said. "There's enough strawberries here to feed the whole holler."

"I know," Mama said. "You and the kids can pick 'em if you want to, and sell 'em."

"Are they ours?"

"Course they're ours. This whole mountaintop is ours now."

I looked around at the honeysuckle and the cabin

and the willow and the wildflowers and strawberries.

"You mean it, Mama? It's ours? The willow tree, too?"

"All of it." Mama smiled and popped a strawberry in her mouth. She looked happy.

"Ain't you sad about Grandpa?" I said.

"Huh!" Mama snorted bitterly. "That old man hated me and made my life miserable. I tried my best to make him love me, but he didn't have it in him. He believed women were wicked and weak and stupid, all of us. So now he's dead, and we're alive!"

"What are we gonna do with all this, Mama?"

"I don't know yet. I'll think about it and talk to Vern about it."

We filled our bucket in about twenty minutes and Mama said, "Let's go in the house."

So we went inside the cabin. It had four rooms all cluttered up with junk and dust and homemade furniture. The first room was a living room and it went straight into the kitchen. Then there were two bedrooms. Mama walked into one of them, and I followed her. It was not a bad room at all. There was a four-poster bed with a patchwork quilt, and a dresser with a mirror.

"This is where you and me slept together every night for three years," Mama said. "Both of us babies."

She sat down on the bed and I sat beside her, and we looked out the window at the weeping willow, which was only a short distance away.

"When the moon was full," Mama said dreamily, "it threw shadows of the willow tree across our bed. We would go to sleep with the willow branches sweeping across our faces. It was nice."

*Willa, Willa, on my pilla'* . . .

"You were born in this bed," Mama went on. "And you were the prettiest baby I ever did see."

"Where did you get my name, Mama?"

"That's always been my secret, Tiny, but you have a right to know. My daddy wouldn't let me call you Ernestina like I wanted to, for Ernest. So I thought of Tina, but I knew he wouldn't hear of that either, so I hit on Tiny—a version of Tina. I knew he would never figure out it came from Ernest's name. So in that small way I defied him."

"Ernestina? That's nice, Mama."

"Don't you like Tiny?"

"Yeah, that's nice, too. It's different. There's a hundred Marys and Susies and Shirleys in school, but there's only one Tiny."

Mama laughed. "And it suits you, too," she said. "There is something very feminine about being tiny, Tiny."

We both laughed.

That laugh sounded nice and it looked nice on Mama's face.

We left the bucket of strawberries on the porch and went back to walking against the sky.

Afterward I remembered that day, not as the day Grandpa died, but as the day Mama came alive.

# ELEVEN

➷ There followed a strange time for me and for my whole family.

Grandpa was buried up on Ruby Mountain under a dogwood tree beside his wife and boy, who died of scarlet fever in 1940.

Vern took me and the boys up on Ruby Mountain every evening for the next two weeks to pick strawberries. Phyllis absolutely refused to pick, and I was too ashamed to knock on people's doors to sell, so we struck up a deal. I picked, she sold, and we split fiftyfifty. We made thirty-two dollars apiece and the boys made more, but, still, buckets of strawberries rotted on the ground.

"Next year we gotta get organized better," Mama

said. "And get some help. What in the world did my daddy do with all them strawberries?"

Mama had a fit of motherhood unequaled in my memory. Most mornings she popped out of bed, cooked breakfast, washed dishes, and started doing things. She made kitchen curtains and couch covers and put up strawberry preserves. I had so many clean clothes I ran out of drawer space, and we discovered windows and mirrors we never knew we had. She planted petunias out beside the house near the Horns', and a small vegetable garden on the hillside.

Very early one Saturday morning, Aunt Evie came out and found Mama looking up at the sun where it was just rising in the east.

"What's the matter, Hazel?" Aunt Evie hollered. "You never been up in time to see the sun in that position before?"

In the past, Mama's feelings would have been hurt, but that day she laughed hard. And Aunt Evie laughed, too. Then the two of them worked in the garden together all morning, and Mama got sunburned. Was this really my mama? It was when I went to the movies one day with Rosemary and Bobby Lynn, and we saw *Invasion of the Body Snatchers* that I finally understood. Yes, I thought, that must be it: my mama's body had been taken over by aliens.

Mama even talked Vern into finishing the fireplace. It looked nice except for that ugly old gun hanging over it.

"Why don't you sell that thing to Mr. Horn and get it over with?" I said to him.

"Sell it!" he bellowed. "Why, that gun went through

the Civil War with my great-granddaddy Vernon Mullins, who was just sixteen and left his right leg over there in the ground in Alexandria. Sell it?"

"Oh," I said, hoping he would shut up. "I see."

"It's a piece of history. It's all that's left of him. That's the trouble with you young people nowadays. You don't appreciate nothing."

And Vern stroked the musket on the wall.

Well, shut my mouth. It was still ugly.

In June the First Annual Black Gap High School Talent Show was held in the auditorium one Friday night. Rosemary had been after me and Bobby Lynn to enter, but we were both plain scared. The three of us went to the talent contest and cheered for Paul Hurley, a senior, who picked a guitar and sang "The Cry of the Wild Goose." All the time I was thinking, "I could beat him."

Paul's picture was in the Black Gap paper the next week with a long list of prizes he won donated by local merchants. I gazed at that picture for hours and read the list of prizes over and over, daydreaming it was me.

When school was out, Mama slept later and we tiptoed around the house with a finger to our lips reminding each other to keep it down. You see, when she went into a cleaning frenzy, she drafted us to help her. It was funny how all those years we wished Mama would get up and do something. Now we wished she would just stay in bed.

One day after Vern came home from work, he called me out of my room into the kitchen, where he and Mama were sitting at the table with a pile of official papers. I sat down.

They stared at me with such strange expressions I glanced down at my shirt to see if everything was buttoned up.

"What'sa matter?" I said.

"Nothing," they said together and looked at each other, then down at the papers.

Well, something was up.

"What's all that stuff?" I said.

"It's your grandpa's will," Mama said. "We didn't know he had one till today, when his lawyer dropped it off."

"Oh."

Vern cleared his throat loudly, but it was Mama who spoke again.

"Remember that day I told you Ruby Mountain was all ours?"

"Yeah, I remember."

"Well, I was wrong. It ain't ours a'tall. It's yours."

"Mine? What d'you mean?"

"He left it all to you," Mama said. "Sixteen and a half acres, but you can't touch it till you're eighteen years old."

"So you own a mountaintop," Vern said.

I was stunned.

Mama laughed.

"Why me?" I said. "He didn't even know me."

"He must have seen you somewhere. He told his lawyer you look like a Lambert, and you talk like a Lambert, and he didn't want no Mullins to git his land."

"So it says here in the will." Vern spoke up. " 'My granddaughter, Tiny Lambert, is my sole hair.' "

"His what?"

"His hair."

"Oh."

I wanted to laugh, but I coughed instead. Vern didn't know about silent letters.

Okay, so I was an heir.

I took a deep breath.

"Wow," I said, and I couldn't think of anything else to say.

Owning Ruby Mountain meant only one thing to me at the moment: the weeping willow was mine.

A few days later, Mr. Horn came over and offered Vern a hundred dollars for his ugly gun.

"Nothin' doin'." Vern laughed. "We're landowners now. And no amount of money will buy that musket."

Mama like to have had a hissy when she heard that. I never heard her talk back to Vern like she did that day.

"Do you know what we could do with a hundred dollars?" she screamed at him.

Then they didn't speak to each other for days. Mama was changing, for sure, and it was unsettling to everybody. Sometimes I went over and talked to Nessie about it, and sometimes I went up to visit Aunt Evie, but most of the time I stayed in my room out of Mama's and Vern's way.

One day when I was cleaning out a dresser drawer, I came across an old valentine I got one time in the third grade. It was one big red heart with the words printed: DO YOU LOVE ME? And there were two boxes, one marked YES and one marked NO. I was supposed to check one box and return the valentine to the sender. The trouble was it wasn't signed, and I never knew who sent it to me. But it gave me an idea: an anonymous love letter to Mr. Gillespie! I could say anything I wanted to say without ever letting him know who I was. And in a sense we would still be communicating. Our minds would touch.

I was so excited I spent hours writing and revising the perfect letter:

*Mr. Gillespie, band director*
*Black Gap, Va.*

*Dear Mr. Gillespie:*
*I have loved you for a very long time, and I am very blue that our love has not ever had a chance to blossom and bloom and if you knew me you would love me also and I will tell you something about myself. I am very tall and I have very long silken curly blond hair, and blue eyes. Some people say I am very pretty. I don't know. I think about you every night before I go to sleep. Will you think of me too?*

*XOXOXOXOXOXOXOXOXOXOXOXOXOXO*
*Ernestina*

I thought that was clever of me to sign it Ernestina. I hid the letter in my clarinet case until I had a chance to go to the coal company store to buy a stamp and mail it.

A week later we started summer band practice on

the field, and I got to see him again. He looked at me like always—like I was just anybody. In a way I was relieved, and in another way I was disappointed. He was cute in his Bermuda shorts.

When we played the marches I was ashamed I hadn't touched my clarinet since school went out. Rosemary was promoted to second clarinet while Bobby Lynn and I stayed at third. I vowed again to practice every day.

When school started, I still had thirty dollars, and this year I planned to have the right clothes. I went to Rosemary for advice.

"What do you reckon I should buy for school?" I asked her.

"Black," she said. "That's the color for this year. Black poodle skirts, slim jims, and black flats with seamless hose."

"Hose?"

I couldn't keep a pair of hose from running to save my life, but I bought two pairs anyway, and a pair of black imitation-suede flats, a black skirt with a pink poodle on it, his gold chain leading to the waist, and a pair of black slim jims.

On the first day of the tenth grade I looked like all the other girls at Black Gap High School, and once again I felt my life had taken a decided turn for the better.

Then one Saturday, when I came home from marching with the band in a parade, there was a surprise waiting for me in the living room: a television set! Mama and everybody else were already hypnotized, so I joined them in watching *The Lone Ranger*. Except for running to the kitchen for food, and going to the bathroom, all of us stayed in the same spot until sign-off time at 11 p.m. We watched *Ted Mack's Original Amateur Hour, My Little Margie*, and *Your Hit Parade*. It was magic.

The next morning I got up real early and went tippy-toeing down the stairs to turn on the set when it signed on. But surprise, surprise, there was Mama and Vern and the boys eating cereal in the living room and watching the test pattern.

It was about that time that Phyllis, who was now eight, started up with a phase of aggravation unprecedented in anybody's memory. She would squeal like a pig when I was trying to watch television or talk on the phone. She would ask the stupidest questions all the time, and follow me around every step I took. She would scoot right up against me on the couch and put her cold dirty feet on me, and she refused to wear socks. I took to pinching her as hard as I could when she got against me like that. Then she would squeal and Mama would yell at me. I just couldn't stand that kid. Sometimes I would give her the silent treatment for days at a time, but that made her worse. My comfort came from Aunt Evie, who assured me that the Lord does not put more on us than we can bear. That was nice to know, but I wondered if the Lord had miscalculated this time.

# TWELVE

When Dolly Horn got married and moved to Princeton, West Virginia, I was the only one who ever paid
any attention to Nessie. The Horns didn't even feed
her regular, and she sat there behind that fence looking
my way all the time. She really loved me, and I loved
her more and more.

I went over there a lot to talk to her through the
fence. She whined and got as close as she could. I
always checked to see if she had fresh water, and most
of the time she didn't. So I gave her water and all the
food I could smuggle to her. Mama and Vern both
fussed if they saw me feeding her.

One day after school I talked to Aunt Evie about

Nessie. We were sitting at her kitchen table playing Old Maid, and eating pumpkin tarts.

"I'm the only one who cares about her," I said. "And I would love to have her. I'll declare it seems like I can't ever have anything I really want. I always have wished for a collie dog, and there Nessie sits all the time pining, and I can't have her. And then there's boys. I want a real boyfriend, somebody cute and popular, and not one boy looks my way."

"Give 'em time, Tiny." Aunt Evie patted my hand. "You're fleshing out real good now. One of these mornings you're gonna look in the mirror and find a pretty woman."

"Sure!"

The very next moment I was sitting there holding the Old Maid.

"See!" I cried. "An ugly Old Maid."

Aunt Evie laughed.

"Bite your tongue!" she said. "Remember what I told you about saying nice things to yourself?"

"It don't work, Aunt Evie."

"Hit does so work!"

Aunt Evie shuffled the cards and dealt another hand.

"Now, Tiny, have you asked Ralph Horn about Nessie?"

"Asked him what?"

"Ask him can you have her. I heard him with my own ears say he'd like to get shed of that dog since Dolly's gone."

"He said that?"

"Yeah, and I'll make you a deal, Miss Pouty-Mouth.

You ask Ralph Horn if you can take Nessie off'n his hands for 'im, and I'll talk to Vern for you."

"You will? What'll you say? He won't listen. It won't do no good. What'll you say?"

"Just listen to yourself." Aunt Evie shook her head. "Never mind what'll I say to Vern. What'll you say to Ralph?"

"I'll be as nice and polite as I know how to be."

"Good," Aunt Evie said. "My Ward useter say sugar draws more flies than vinegar. And hit's the God's truth."

Then Aunt Evie was left holding the Old Maid. We laughed.

"Yeah, there I am," she said. "I'm the Old Maid for sure."

I dealt, and we played in earnest silence for a few minutes.

"What is 'happily ever after,' Aunt Evie?" I finally said. "Does it exist?"

"Yes, Tiny. I never found hit, my own self, but I know hit exists. If I could have married my Ward . . ."

When I went back home and into the kitchen, Vern was sitting at the table in his underwear. A bottle of bourbon was in front of him, and he was holding a glass half-full.

I went to the refrigerator and poured myself some milk. Then I stood looking out the window over the sink, not even thinking of Vern Mullins.

"What'sa matter?" he said, and I could tell, the way he was slurring his words, he was nearly drunk. "You never saw a man in his drawers before?"

Not but about five thousand times, I was thinking,

but I could see he was in no mood to be sassed. I turned around and looked at him.

"Sure I have."

"When?"

I shrugged. "Lotsa times."

"Who?"

"Well, you. Who else?"

Vern laughed. I forced myself to smile at him and set my glass in the sink. Then I started to walk by him to the living room. That's when he grabbed me hard around the waist and plopped me down solid on his lap. I struggled, but his grip was tight.

"Let me go, Vern."

"Just set still a minute and talk to your daddy. I don't never get to see you."

I was thinking, *You're not my daddy, and I'm glad you're not!* But I didn't say it. I sat still, but I didn't relax. His old breath smelled awful as he blew it in my face.

"How's high school?" he said.

*What a stupid thing to say*, I was thinking.

"Fine," I said.

He started rubbing my thigh with his right hand while he held me in place with his left.

"Vern, let me go," I said.

"Just set still like I told you!"

He belched real big. Then he put his hand under my dress, and I made one powerful lunge out of his reach. He started laughing—snorting, I should say— and that made me so mad I couldn't see straight. I went into the living room where Mama was sitting writing something in a book. She kept a list of all the things she saw advertised on television that she wanted to buy at the A & P.

"Dee—eep Magic," the television was babbling from the corner like an insane relative. "The cleansing lotion that cleans your skin deep, deep down where beauty begins."

"Why do you stay with him?" I hissed at her, as I flopped down on the couch beside Mama.

"What're you talking about?" she snapped back.

"I hate him!"

"Who?"

"That good-for-nothing man you married! I hate—"

But there was no finishing that sentence. Mama was all over me like a mad woman. She slapped me first, then she grabbed me up by the shoulders and shook me till I saw stars.

"Don't you never, never say that to me again!" she hollered in my face. "As good as Vern's been to you! You should fall down on your knees and thank God for your stepdaddy!"

She was panting and all red in the face. There was a ringing in my ears. We just stood there glaring at each other for a minute, then I spun around on my heels and rushed upstairs. My head was confused and reeling. I didn't know whether to cry, or fume and fuss some more. Worse yet, maybe Mama was right and there was something wrong with me that I didn't appreciate Vern for all he did for us. I went into my room where Phyllis was playing paper dolls. Couldn't I just get away from everybody? Was there no place I could be alone?

"What'sa matter?" Phyllis said.

I flopped down on the bed.

"Get out!" I yelled at her.

"Make me!" she yelled back.

But I couldn't make anybody do anything. I was helpless. I dissolved in tears.

# THIRTEEN

⋊ The next morning, Mama was watching Dave Garroway when I came down for breakfast. I went to the kitchen and fixed myself a bowl of corn flakes, and she came in and sat down at the table with a cup of coffee.

"I reckon I shouldn't have slapped you," she said. "What did Vern do to you?"

"Nothin'."

"Why was you so mad?"

"He was drunk."

"Huh! He's drunk a lot. So what else is new?"

I shrugged again. What was the use?

"I don't know what I would do without him," she said, and her voice quivered.

I looked at her and there were tears in her eyes.

"How could I feed you and the young'uns? Did you ever think of that, huh? This is Vern's house. Where would we go?"

She was terrified.

"I don't know, Mama, but it sounds like you've been thinking about it."

"The thought has crossed my mind, Tiny, but it just crossed and kept on going. How can I make a living and raise four kids at the same time? I've got no education. What can I do?"

I guess that was the truth. Lord knows we had little enough as it was with Vern bringing home good money from the mines. And there was no way we would ever get a penny out of him if Mama left him.

"Well, quit worrying about it. I'll just stay out of his way."

"Did he pinch you or what?"

"Yeah, he pinched me."

"I'll tell him to stop treating you like a child. He forgets you're growing up."

Now, that was a laugh, but I didn't feel like laughing.

Mama changed the subject quickly.

"You put me in mind a whole lot of that Betty Anderson on *Father Knows Best*, Tiny, except you're not as tall. Why don't you put up your hair in a ponytail?"

I had been thinking of doing that.

"Maybe I will. It needs to grow some more."

"Yeah," she agreed.

We didn't speak of Vern again for a long time after that. I decided it was best to just stay clear of him, so I wouldn't have to worry Mama. He was my problem.

A few days later, Aunt Evie asked Vern about Nessie, but it was like talking to a wall. And Mr. Horn wouldn't even hear me out. So much for sugar being better than vinegar.

I sent a Christmas card to Mr. Gillespie and put XO's all over it, and signed it *Ernestina*. Then I kissed it before I put it in the mail. That was a week before Christmas.

On the night before Christmas Eve, Beau trapped me in the kitchen and wouldn't let me go till I agreed to read *A Christmas Carol* with him aloud. He just loved culture, Beau did. So I settled down seriously with him at the kitchen table, which was cluttered with dirty dishes.

"I wear the chains I forged in life," Beau said, his voice an ominous, ghostly quiver. Sometimes he was a really good actor, and the kitchen was deadly quiet except for his hoarse whisper as Marley's ghost. Then there was a sudden rattle at the kitchen door and I nearly jumped through the air.

"What was that?" I whispered.

"Just a piece of undigested beef," Beau said in his Scrooge voice, "or a bit of mustard."

"No, really, Beau, somebody's at the door."

"Nobody's at the door, Tiny."

There came a sharp bark at the door.

"Nessie!" I rushed out and there she was panting and swishing her tail like a whisk broom, and jumping all over me. I threw my arms around her.

"Oh, Nessie!"

How good it was to hold her. She came into the house with me.

"Uh-oh!" Beau said. "You better not let Daddy see it."

"She is not an it."

I stroked her softly, and she snuggled against me.

Phyllis came in from the living room. "Lassie!" She laughed and hugged Nessie. "Ain't she pretty?"

"Shh . . ." I said. "It's Nessie, not Lassie. Where's Vern?"

"Watching *Gunsmoke* with Mama. Let's hide her upstairs."

"Let's finish this chapter," Beau said irritably.

But Nessie wanted all my attention. I gave her a piece of bologna. That's when somebody knocked on the door.

"Where's my dawg?" came a muffled voice. "You got my dawg in there?"

It was Mr. Horn, of course. Nessie whimpered and slunk into a corner.

I let Mr. Horn in.

"Hidy, Mr. Horn," Beau said. "How ya doin'? Lose something?"

"You know I did. Where's my dawg?"

Then his eye fell on poor Nessie. With two big steps he was across the room and gave a mighty yank on her collar.

"Come on, ya bitch!"

Nessie let out a yelp, and I flinched.

"Oh, don't hurt her!" Phyllis said, and threw her arms around Nessie, which like to have surprised me to death. I never thought Phyllis had it in her to love anybody but herself.

"Git out'n my way," Mr. Horn hollered.

He started pulling Nessie toward the door, and she whimpered.

Vern came in from the living room to see what all the fuss was about.

"What'n the world?" he said.

"Vernon Mullins, I come to git my dawg," Mr. Horn said.

"Well, take yer damn dawg and good riddance!" Vern said.

"She came looking for me!" I screamed above the commotion. I was exasperated. "Nobody cares about her but me! How come y'all can't see that? How come I can't have her!"

For about five seconds there was silence in the room, and all eyes were on me. Then the two men glanced at each other and Mr. Horn led Nessie out the door. I left the kitchen abruptly and headed for my room.

"I wear the chains I forged in life!" Beau hollered and threw the book after me.

The next day it came a freezing rain that turned to sleet. The kids were all excited about Christmas, and hoped the sleet would turn to snow. Try as I might, I couldn't get Nessie off my mind. I would look over there and see her standing, shivering in the sleet and looking toward our house. She was pitiful.

Then she got out of the gate again, and Mr. Horn put her back and tied her to the fence. That broke my heart. She couldn't even reach her house from where he tied her. She stood there in the weather, waiting for me to save her. How could I possibly stand that?

Beau, Luther, and Phyllis all went to bed early because it was Christmas Eve. I stayed up with Mama and Vern to watch television, but I couldn't tell you a thing I saw. The image of poor Nessie standing there shivering in the sleet was emblazoned in front of my eyeballs. When I went up to go to bed with Phyllis, I looked out the window with dread in my heart.

And there she was. I felt like it was me standing there in the wet and cold looking for somebody to love me. She couldn't lie down on the soaked ground and she couldn't reach her house. Her head was bowed close to the ground, but she was facing my house.

I crawled in bed beside Phyllis.

"Please, God, help Nessie," I whispered in the dark. "Help me to help Nessie."

"Steal her!" a voice came back.

I jumped, but it was Phyllis, of course.

"What'n the world you doing awake, Phyllis? Santy Claus won't come if you're awake."

"How can I sleep with Nessie standing out there?" she said.

There for a minute I almost liked her.

"I guess she'll be all right, Phyllis. We gotta stop thinking about her."

"I been trying to stop, but I can't. The Horns are so mean to her."

I tiptoed to the window again and looked out. I could barely see the sad figure bowed down in the cold. Phyllis came up beside me.

"Let's steal her, Tiny," she said again.

"And what good would that do? Mr. Horn would just come and get her, and what's more, we would be in trouble."

"He's in bed now. And Nessie could be warm and dry on Christmas Eve."

I looked at Phyllis and saw that her eyes were sparkling with excitement. Yeah, I thought, everybody must be asleep by now. We could bring Nessie up here in our room and dry her, give her something to eat, pet her. I glanced out the window again. The sleet was turning to snow. My mind was made up.

"Okay, let's do it."

Suddenly the room was electric.

"We have to do everything without lights. First our shoes and socks and coats and scarves," I whispered.

We didn't speak as we donned our heavy gear over our pajamas in the dark.

I sat down on the edge of the bed, and she sat down beside me. "We have to be as quiet as can be. If anybody hears us, it'll all be over."

"Okay."

"Now, you stay behind me going out. Coming back in, you hold the gate and the door for me and Nessie."

"Okay."

I took a deep breath, and opened the door. All was black and quiet. We tiptoed down the stairs. Phyllis held on to my coat, and I could hear her breathing excitedly. At the front door we had to be extra careful because it was liable to squeak real bad. But we managed to ease outside without a sound. Then we went down the tall steps, all the time Phyllis hanging on to me without a sound.

When we were in the open yard without shelter, we discovered just how cold it was. Big icy flakes of snow were falling. We headed toward the Horns' gate. About that time Nessie saw us coming, and she started shaking all over. She was happy! I was afraid she would bark, but she didn't, the sweet thing. She just jumped around a lot. We crept in the gate and went to her. My hands were too cold to feel the catch and I fumbled with her chain. Then I discovered to my horror that the chain was so tight around her neck I couldn't get one finger underneath it. Tears came to my eyes.

"Be still," I said softly to her and stroked her cold, wet body. "We're going to help you."

Phyllis held her as I struggled with the chain. At last I found the catch and unsnapped it. She was free. We didn't have to urge her to come with us. We turned silently, heading home, and she followed happily.

Snow had covered us all by that time, and stung our faces as we walked against the wind. We didn't speak as we went up the tall steps and gently opened the front door. There we stopped and listened. The only sound was Vern's snoring, which was a relief. Together we guided Nessie into the dark house and up the stairs. All went well. At last we were in our room, with the door closed tightly behind us.

"We made it," Phyllis whispered excitedly.

"So far, so good," I said. "But I know she's hungry and thirsty. I'm going to find her something."

We shed our heavy clothing, and Nessie settled on a rug beside our bed. She sighed heavily and rested her chin on her paws. Phyllis covered her with a quilt.

I went down to the kitchen and filled an empty lard bucket half-full of water, and some leftover pork and cabbage with corn bread crumbled up in it. When I took it upstairs, Phyllis was rubbing Nessie with an old flannel shirt.

"She's soaked to the skin," she said.

I set the food and water down for Nessie, and she gobbled it up.

"We can't hide her for long," I said.

We wrapped up in blankets and settled on the floor, one on either side of her.

"I'm going to beg Daddy for her," Phyllis said.

Yeah, that was a thought: Phyllis. Vern would do just about anything for her.

"We better go to bed, Phyllis," I said. "Or Santy Claus will never come."

"Well, I don't believe that stuff no more, Tiny."

"You don't? How come?"

"That's kid stuff."

We were quiet in our own thoughts for a long time. I was thinking I never really saw Phyllis as a person before. She was this aggravating, squealing young'un I had to put up with. But there might be a real person in there.

Nessie slept peacefully.

Finally we crawled into bed, Phyllis and I. It was about two, I reckoned. Phyllis curled up to me, and put her dirty feet on me, and I didn't mind much. It was very cold, and we went to sleep fitting together like two spoons.

# FOURTEEN

⨂ Sometime during the night, Nessie crawled into bed with us and snuggled up to my back so that I was wedged between her and Phyllis like a bug in a rug. We were sleeping soundly and didn't hear everybody else tumbling around making Christmas-morning noises all over the house. Then our door flew open and Beau bellowed, "Come on, lazybones, it's Christmas —holy hot dog!"

I felt Nessie's head shoot up and her tail started wagging. She made the whole bed shake.

"Shut the door!" Phyllis said.

Beau stepped inside and closed the door.

"You're gonna be in trouble!" he said, grinning wickedly.

"You open your big mouth, and I'll tell you-know-what," Phyllis said.

Beau's grin faded.

"Well, how you gonna keep that cow hid?" he said.

Nessie slid off the bed and went to him. He started petting her.

"It ain't so bad," he said, referring to Nessie.

Then the door flew open again, and in walked Vern.

"Come on down and see what Santy brung you!" he hollered, loud with Christmas cheer. He had a drink in his hand. "What the hell . . . ?"

Nessie, not knowing any better, went to Vern, wagging her tail.

We didn't say anything. Vern's face took on a puzzled look. Our game was up.

"Daddy, if you take Nessie back to Mr. Horn, I will die," Phyllis announced.

Vern looked at her.

"I will die," she repeated.

Nessie came back to the side of the bed.

"But before I die, I will not ever speak to you again."

Beau giggled, then quickly clamped his hand over his mouth. Luther appeared in the doorway.

"Uh-oh," he said.

"I will squeal so loud . . ." Phyllis continued.

"Just shut up," Vern said at last. "Whose big idea was this anyway?"

"Mine," Phyllis said.

"You lie!" Luther said. "You know it was Tiny's!"

"It was my idea, and I will squeal until I die if you take her back," Phyllis said.

"You can start any time now," Vern said. "'Cause she's going back."

Well, Phyllis did start squealing. She squealed so long and so shrill that Nessie tried to crawl under the bed, but she was too big. Beau and Luther abruptly left the room and Vern stood there. He didn't know what to do. Directly, he turned and left the room, too.

Phyllis shut up immediately and turned to me and grinned a big toothy grin. She was amazing.

Nessie jumped back up on our bed between us.

Then Mama came in.

"Now, girls," she said. "Y'all know this won't do. You might just as well take that dog back now."

"No," Phyllis said emphatically. "Never."

Mama put her hands on her hips and glared at Phyllis. Phyllis sat up in bed, put her own hands on her hips, and glared right back. All I had to do was lie back and watch. It wasn't half bad having Phyllis on my side for a change, I thought, fighting my battles for me.

Phyllis won that round. Mama left the room in defeat. We tumbled out of bed and put on our britches and sweaters. I put on socks and shoes, too, but Phyllis, of course, went barefooted as usual. I didn't mention it. No need to stir her up now. Taking Nessie along, we went down to open our presents. There was a foot of snow outside, and the hills were brilliant and sparkling in the morning sun.

There were presents piled all over the place, and suddenly I was excited. Nessie bounced around like she had good sense.

Such a Christmas! I thought.

Mama silently handed out presents. She was mad. Vern was nowhere to be seen and I guessed he was next door talking to Mr. Horn.

I got a white Banlon cardigan from Mama and a black wool pleated skirt from Vern, a package of pony-tail holders in assorted colors from Phyllis and a pocketbook from Beau and Luther. I was opening up my last package when Vern walked in and stood there looking at us in silence. He had his hands in his overall pockets, which meant he had something heavy on his mind. Everybody, even Nessie, got quiet and looked at him. He cleared his throat.

"Well, Phyllis, Tiny . . ." he said, and stopped.

"Did you talk to Mr. Horn?" Phyllis asked.

"Yes, I did," Vern said. "And he wants his dog back right now."

With that, Phyllis went into her squealing routine again. It was almost more than anyone could bear. Mama and I covered our ears, Beau and Luther cussed, but you couldn't hear them over the din, Nessie wiggled behind the couch, and Vern looked pained. I felt a little sorry for him.

Suddenly he went to the fireplace, plucked the old Civil War musket off the wall, and marched back outside. Phyllis was shocked into silence, and a ringing reverberated where her screech had been. We all gaped at each other.

"What . . . ?"

"Do you reckon . . . ?"

"Naw, it can't be."

But it was. About two minutes later, Vern came back in empty-handed.

"Merry Christmas," he muttered. "You got yourselfs a dawg."

Phyllis flew into her daddy's arms and covered him with kisses. I could only stand there in complete shock, afraid to believe.

"And you can't thank the old man?" Vern teased me, grinning.

I looked at Mama and she was grinning, too. It was really true. Vern had traded his gun for Nessie. I kissed Vern on the cheek.

"Thanks."

Then I went crawling behind the couch calling Nessie.

I volunteered to clean up the kitchen after breakfast while everybody else watched the Mormon Tabernacle Choir on the television. Nessie stayed right with me, half the time under my feet. Then Vern came in and poured himself another glass of bourbon.

"This is the best Christmas I ever had, Vern," I said to him.

He put his arm across my shoulder.

"You're growing up to be such a pretty thing," he said. "You know I love you, Tiny."

I giggled, feeling nervous and uncomfortable.

"I mean it," he said seriously.

Then he kissed me on the cheek.

"I love you," he said again.

# FIFTEEN

⤳ There followed wonderful and happy days, close
days for me and my sister. We spent all our free time
together with Nessie, washing her in the bathtub when
Vern was gone, teaching her tricks like fetch-if-you-
feel-like-it, and most of the time she didn't. "Sit" and
"stay," to Nessie, both meant roll over, and she did
that perfectly. We sometimes laughed at her till we
cried, and she laughed with us.

I found out Phyllis would do reasonable things like
wear her socks and shoes if I was nice to her, and that
Christmas morning when Nessie came to us was the
last time we ever heard Phyllis squeal like a pig.

Sometimes on Sundays, Vern took us up on Ruby
Mountain, where we ran and ran across the windy

mountaintop. We holed up in the log cabin and did girl things like comb each other's hair and paint each other's fingernails.

We crept up under the weeping willow away from the world and made up stories about long ago and far away. And always between us there was Nessie, agreeable and lovable, swishing her tail. We brushed her and cleaned the burrs out of her coat, scratched her belly and kissed her nose. We spoiled her to pieces and she loved us.

In April the mountains came alive with color and sweet smells, with wild buttercups and lilacs, apple and cherry and dogwood trees, and all kinds of wildflowers.

Then one day I heard Phyllis talking on the phone to one of her classmates, and she said, "When I grow up I want to be just like my big sister, and I want to look like her, too."

I was surprised and pleased. I looked at myself in the mirror and blushed a little. Yes, I had changed some for the better.

Still nobody called me up and asked me for a date. Bobby Lynn dated somebody different every weekend, and Rosemary started going steady with Roy Woodrow Viers, who played the tuba. You couldn't have pried those two apart with a crowbar.

In May, I turned sixteen and the strawberries came on like crazy. You never saw the beat. Aunt Evie and Cecil Hess and all the little Hesses helped us pick for a share of the profits. Cecil loved to tease me about my ponytail. He would grab on to it and say, "Giddy up!" Aunt Evie would wink knowingly at me, but I laughed at her. I knew he was just being Cecil, as likable as always, and as sweet to Phyllis, Beau, and Luther as he was to his own brothers and sisters. Cecil was on the junior varsity football team that year, but the next fall, which would be our junior year, he was to move up to the varsity. Maybe by then I would be playing first clarinet.

About this time it was rumored that Mr. Gillespie had a girlfriend in a college in North Carolina, but I didn't believe it. He wouldn't. I still fantasized and wrote anonymous letters to him.

Then it was time for the second annual talent show. I felt so good I let Bobby Lynn talk me into entering with her. On a Friday after school we met in the auditorium with the other contestants for the first time to discuss what we were going to do. Only a few holler kids showed, but all the town kids were there—some singers and some pianists, some guitarists and some comedians.

There was also a four-piece rock group led by Geezer Coleman. Carole Ann Hudson was going to do a dramatic reading from *Anastasia*, and Lois Harmon was doing her baton routine with the fire on the ends and all. The Mountain Dew Drops, a bluegrass band, was there, and everybody was embarrassed for them because bluegrass music simply was not in style anymore.

But the one who worried me most was Connie Collins. Her act was tap and ballet, and she took dance lessons in Bristol every Saturday. Even though Connie was as dumb as a coal bucket, she was rich and she looked just like Marilyn Monroe. The Collinses had the grandest house in town because they owned the liquor store.

As for singing, Bobby Lynn whispered to me that I had no competition. Still, I wondered if I was good enough to beat all those town kids. What had I got myself into? When my name was called, I bolted clear out of my seat, and somebody giggled. My face went hot and Bobby Lynn stood up beside me.

"Tiny is going to sing," she said sweetly. "I am going to accompany her on the piano. And I am going to yodel."

All eyes were on me, and I didn't say a word. I felt so stupid and inferior. They're smirking, I thought. They don't think I can sing a lick.

"First rehearsal is Tuesday afternoon at three-thirty," Mrs. Miller was saying. "Death is the only excuse I'll accept, and then you better have a death certificate."

Ha. Ha.

The meeting broke up, and we walked outside. It was such a perfect, perfect day, and the air smelled fresh and sweet. My spirits were lifted.

"Let's walk down to the shop," Bobby Lynn said. "You gotta see the new bathing suits. They are so cute!"

She was speaking of the Black Gap Style Shoppe on Main Street, where her mother worked. They had all the latest fashions from Bristol. The new county swimming pool was almost ready for its grand opening, and everybody was looking at bathing suits these days.

Mrs. Clevinger smiled at us when we went in the

shop. I had met her at ball games. She was petite and dimpled like Bobby Lynn, and you wouldn't believe she was almost thirty-five years old. The one thing wrong with her was her marital status, which was not respectable, if I could believe the rumors at school. Bobby Lynn seemed ashamed of whatever was going on in her house because she had never discussed it with me, but rumor had it that Mr. Clevinger had recently moved out. I didn't know another soul who was divorced except Mama's friend Dixie, and nobody with any sense would stay married to Dixie.

"Show Tiny the new bathing suits," Bobby Lynn said to her mother.

"Oh, my goodness, yes!" Mrs. Clevinger bubbled. "That little pokey-dotted one. Won't she be sweet in it?"

Bobby Lynn squealed, and they both giggled.

They were the cutest bathing suits I ever had laid eyes on, but the little pokey-dotted one Mrs. Clevinger mentioned was my favorite. In a minute I was behind the curtains trying it on. When I came out, Mrs. Clevinger and Bobby Lynn ooed and ahed. Then Connie Collins walked in. Without a word, she towered over me like a tree and looked down her nose.

I turned around and around in front of the mirror, almost afraid to believe my eyes. I had grown an inch or two taller, my hair was longer and shinier, it seemed, and I was rounder in all the right places. Why, I looked almost . . . well . . . nearly . . . why I did! I looked good! The suit was a strapless one-piece, blue with white pokey dots and these two cute little ruffles on the butt.

"You are gorgeous!" Bobby Lynn said.

I loved her.

"Well, I would take off those silly ruffles!" Connie said sharply.

Connie had the most beautiful clothes of anybody I knew, but there for a minute I would swear she acted like she was jealous. That tickled me more than anything, and I was bound and determined I would have that suit.

"Take the ruffles off? Goodness no!" Mrs. Clevinger said. "Those ruffles will be the main attraction at the new county swimming pool. You're a doll, Tiny."

Connie turned quickly and pretended to be very interested in a red sundress. Mrs. Clevinger winked at me, and Bobby Lynn giggled.

As it turned out, that bathing suit cost $9.98! That made me swallow hard, but I would have it. My strawberry money was tucked away in an old coat pocket in the back of my closet at home, and Mrs. Clevinger put the bathing suit on her own account till I could get the money to her.

I hired a taxi to take me home because I was too excited to wait the two hours for Mama and Vern to meet me, like we planned, at the A & P when they came to do the shopping. I couldn't wait that long for Mama and Phyllis to see my new bathing suit.

The taxi driver was Rosemary's cousin, Gary Dean Layne, and he tried to flirt with me on the way home. He was at least nineteen, and I sure wasn't interested in anybody that old except Mr. Gillespie, but I was getting the big head. I wondered if I would ever feel inferior to anybody again. Gary Dean charged me only forty cents when it was supposed to be fifty cents. I bounded into the house calling for Mama and Phyllis, but nobody was there, not even Nessie.

Well, shucks, I thought, they must have all gone strawberry picking. I went upstairs and put on my bathing suit anyway. They would see me first thing when they got home. For a while I pranced around in front of the mirror singing into an invisible microphone, and dancing. Then I took a jar of peanut butter and 'nilla wafers from the kitchen and settled down to watch the last of *American Bandstand*. Justine was dancing the waltz with a new partner, and Johnny Mathis was singing a love song.

I closed my eyes.

Me and Mr. Gillespie are at the swimming pool on opening day. He volunteers to teach me how to swim. I know he is totally overcome by my new bathing suit. He suggests I enter the beauty contest next year.

When I heard the pickup coming up the hill, I thought it was everybody coming back from Ruby Mountain, but it was only Vern who walked in the door. He was swaying.

"Where's Mama and the young'uns?" I said to him.

"Cecil drove 'em up in his daddy's truck to pick strawberries," Vern said, slurring his words.

He was drunker than usual for that time of day. I sat perfectly still, stared straight ahead at the television, and folded my arms across my chest, hoping he wouldn't notice what I was wearing.

"I went to see my daddy," Vern said. "He's in the hospital."

I still didn't say anything, or move. Somewhere I could hear warning bells. Danger. Look out.

*American Bandstand* went off. It was time for *Howdy Doody.*

"What'cha got on?" Vern said, and my heart dropped like a rock.

"Just a suit," I said.

"Well, it's new, ain't it?"

"Sorta."

"Stand up and let me look at it."

"Oh, Vern . . ."

"Stand up!"

Obediently I stood up and held my arms rigidly to my sides, my palms cupping my thighs. I glanced at him, thinking if he would move out of the door I would run out and go up to Aunt Evie's. But Vern was looking at me and he wasn't moving at all.

"Hold your arms out and turn around," he said.

I did as he said, feeling my face go hot with shame. Oh, God . . .

On television, Buffalo Bob was saying, "Hey kids, do you know what time it is?"

And Vern grabbed me.

# SIXTEEN

⋟ I am dreaming and it is nice. I am only a baby two years old, and Willa is with me, and my real daddy, Ernest Bevins, is there, too, and oh, we are having so much fun in the wildflowers up on Ruby Mountain. Willa and my daddy are so lovely with their curly red hair against the blue sky, and I think yes, yes, I guess I will just stay right here forever with Willa and my daddy and never grow up because growing up hurts and bad things happen to you.

My daddy has eyes like blue ice as he lifts me high above his head into the wind and I giggle and gurgle like babies do. Willa is picking daisies and going, "Loves me . . . loves me not . . ." in a singsong baby voice while her red hair flows away into the grass and

into the mountain spring. Then we are all eating peanut butter and 'nilla wafers. But they don't taste good.
They stink like bourbon.

Suddenly I look at my daddy and I am filled with
rage.

"Where have you been?" I scream at him. "You
should have been here to look after me!"

He is very sad, but I am mad and I want to hurt
him. I throw a rock at him and it hits him in the eye.

"Tell your mother," he says to me.

Blood pours out on the ground from his eye and
Willa runs away crying. I have never seen Willa cry
before.

"Oh, come back, Willa!" I call after her. "Come
back!"

"Tell your mother," Daddy says again.

I woke up crying in the warm May night. Oh, Willa
. . . come back!

Phyllis turned over in her sleep and mumbled something about strawberries. Nessie sighed where she was
sleeping under the window.

Willa . . . come back.

The words echoed in my head like a sad melody.

> *Willa, Willa, on my pilla',*
> *Come in your pretty lace*
> *And your pink face.*

First her sweet fragrance flooded my room; then she
appeared in a rush of color.

"Oh, Willa . . ."

Her bright red hair lay in wispy folds all down her

back and onto the floor when she knelt beside my bed. Her eyes were as stormy gray as a snow sky in her petal-pink face. She was wearing a mint-green satin dress and she was so lovely in her aura of goodness she glowed in the dark.

"Hush," she said sweetly and dried my tears with her hair. "I'll be here as long as you need me."

*Dear Mr. Gillespie:*

*I have a friend her name is Willa and a man hurt her. Now she doesn't want to get up or go to school or talk to anybody. She wants to be alone all the time, and she cries at night. I am afraid she is losing her mind. I wish you were here to tell me why this happened. Why did God let this happen to my friend? I wish you could tell me so I can make her understand.*

*Love, Ernestina*

I missed the talent show rehearsal, then pulled out completely with no explanation to Bobby Lynn. I should have told her something, I guess, but it didn't matter. Bobby Lynn was mad and stopped speaking to me, but that didn't matter either. Cecil was the only person who asked me what was wrong. It was when he found me sitting alone in a corner of the auditorium.

"Nothing's wrong," was all he got out of me.

*Dear Mr. Gillespie:*

*Willa says she wishes she was dead. She feels dirty and ashamed. She says she can't think of a good reason to go on living. If you are wondering why Willa won't tell, well, it is because he said he would kill her dog, and he will too. She loves her dog. Oh, Mr. Gillespie, it is so hard to be hurt so bad.*

*Love, Ernestina*

In band, I was afraid to look straight at Mr. Gillespie. I was afraid he would see something in my eyes. But one day, without warning, he said, "I have something to say to Ernestina."

"Who?" somebody said.

I felt all the blood leave my face, and I looked toward him, but not directly at him. Was he looking at me? No, he was not looking at me.

"I am very distressed," he continued, and his voice trembled a little.

Who else besides Mr. Gillespie would ever say, "I am very distressed"?

"What about?" somebody said.

"Willa must tell her mother," Mr. Gillespie went on. "It is urgent. She must."

"Excuse me, Mr. Gillespie," Jimmy Ted O'Quinn said with exaggerated politeness, "but what are you talking about?"

My heart was beating so hard I was afraid somebody would see it or hear it.

"I am not speaking to you, Jimmy Ted," Mr. Gillespie said. "The person I am addressing knows what I mean. She also must know I am her friend, and she can come to me anytime, in strictest confidence."

There was silence in the band room for the first time

ever as Mr. Gillespie looked around the room slowly with a very sad look on his face.

"Okay," he said at last, and raised his arms. *"Die Fledermaus."*

*June 1958*
*Dear Mr. Gillespie:*
*Thank you for what you said in band. But I do not want you to be very distressed. What you said helped me a whole lot, and I feel better. I appreciate your concern.*

*Love, Ernestina*

*P.S. I will tell Willa.*

How could I face Mr. Gillespie after all the lovey-dovey stuff I said to him in my earlier letters? I could never tell him.

Bobby Lynn won first place in the talent contest with her yodeling. I didn't even remember to go to the show, but I saw her picture in the paper with all the prizes she won. She was smiling and happy. Aunt Evie brought the paper to me. She was proud of Bobby Lynn.

Mr. Gillespie went to Lexington to get married at the end of June.

I didn't write to him again. There was nothing left to say to him.

In my next dream, Grandpa Lambert is there. He is mad at Mama for marrying Vern. His eyes are little red-hot coals like in the fireplace, and he has awful wrinkles on his face, and he cusses Mama, and he cusses me. Then he turns into Grandma Mullins, Vern's mama who died. She laughs at me.

"You thought you were hot stuff in that bathing suit!" she says. "You shoulda took off the ruffles like I told you. Ruffles are dangerous."

And she smirks and laughs. She wins. Even when she's dead she can beat me. I hate her and I hate Vern.

I woke up. It was the dead of night and Phyllis was out cold. My window was open and I could hear the frogs croaking down in the creek. I could see the hills silhouetted against a jeweled sky. I pictured the people all sleeping in their beds up and down the holler just like they had always done. They couldn't imagine the awful thing that had happened.

I wanted to get up and take another bath, but Mama was mad at me for taking all those baths lately. It was hot and very late, and I was thirsty. I sat up, and Nessie lifted her head and started slapping her tail against the bed. I patted her.

I thought there might be one Red Rock Cola in the refrigerator. I would sneak down the stairs and get it. I stepped out into the hall and closed my door so Nessie couldn't follow me. I could hear Vern snoring. I tiptoed down the stairs and into the kitchen. Yes, there was the Red Rock. I opened it quietly and tiptoed back toward the stairs. At the bottom of the stairs I paused because there in the living room I could see a cigarette glowing in the dark.

"Mama?"

Silence.

"Why are you sitting in the dark, Mama?"

"I couldn't sleep. Go back to bed, Tiny."

I had avoided Mama. I had not even looked in her eyes all these weeks because I felt I could never tell her. Even that first night, when I said I had a headache and begged off going to the A & P, she did not ask me a single question. If she sensed something was wrong, she did not mention it. Maybe she did not admit any suspicions even to herself. Maybe she had no suspicions. As I hesitated there at the foot of the stairs, I envisioned going to her in the dark and curling up beside her and crying in her arms like a little girl. Maybe I could tell her . . .

"Mama?"

"For Pete's sake, Tiny!" she snapped. "Can't I never be alone?"

Without another word I went upstairs and back to my room.

Phyllis had sprawled herself all over the bed, and she was snoring just like Vern. I poked her real hard with my elbow.

"Oh!" she said, jumping up. "What'd you do that for?"

"Move your butt over!"

"Well, you didn't have to poke me so hard! That hurt!"

I turned my back to her.

"You know something, Tiny?" she said angrily. "I don't like you no more!"

"Well, so what? I don't like you neither!"

# SEVENTEEN

⚜ The blue-and-white pokey-dotted bathing suit lay all wadded up in a knot and pushed to the back of the bottom drawer in my dresser. I never wanted to see it again and I didn't go swimming at the new county pool. The summer sorta ran together in a blur. I think it rained all the time.

In my mind I killed Vern.

Mama grew quiet, and Phyllis was quiet, too, for a change.

The boys spent a lot of time with Cecil.

I spent all my time with Nessie and Willa. We made up a whole fantasy world that summer, Willa and I did. I think there were unicorns. It was a way to get out of the real world. It didn't matter.

Rosemary called me often. She and Roy were concerned about me. They got me a blind date with Roy's cousin, but I wouldn't go. Bobby Lynn finally got over her mad spell when she forgot what it was she was mad about, and she started calling me again. We were going into our junior year and we all moved up to first clarinet in summer band practice, but it wasn't important anymore.

When school started, I hung out with Bobby Lynn and Rosemary as always at stroll-and-perch time. Roy had been a part of our group since last school year; then one morning, out of the blue, Cecil came over and started hanging out with our crowd. After that he was with us every day. I think he had a crush on Bobby Lynn, but whatever his reasons I was proud to have him with us because he had become a very important football player—an overnight sensation. His name was in the paper every week. And he was *my* neighbor.

The last week in October, Bobby Lynn invited me to spend the night at her house, and Mama said it was okay. I decided I would go because I hadn't done anything out of the ordinary for a long time. Though I had been to Bobby Lynn's house a few times, I had never spent the night. She lived right off Main Street and we walked down there after school on Friday. There were golden leaves all over the sidewalk and little gusts of wind swirled them around our feet. We kicked at them and laughed, and breathed in the crisp autumn air.

Bobby Lynn's house was small and made of white boards, with a low brick wall running around it, and a cute brick walkway from the gate to the front door.

We went in and tossed our books on the couch. It was cozy in there with five rooms all jumbled together, flowered curtains and couch covers to match, doilies on everything, family pictures everywhere, and a piano!

We ate Jell-O with bananas and nuts in it, then she sat down at the piano. She played by ear. Bobby Lynn had told me that when she was in grade school she had taken piano lessons for a few years, but she wouldn't follow directions or practice scales or anything, and her teacher got so exasperated she gave up. She just sat there and let Bobby Lynn play for fun. And that's when she really learned to play. She could play anything from "Honky Tonk Angel" to Mozart. All she needed to do was hear a tune a few times and she could play it. I could sing a few bars of anything and she had it. We were doing "The Rock And Roll Waltz" when Bobby Lynn's mama came in from work and dropped down in an armchair beside me.

*One, two and then rock,*
*One, two and then roll,*
*They did The Rock And Roll Waltz.*

At first Mrs. Clevinger just listened, then she started clapping in time. Then we did the chorus again while Mrs. Clevinger and I hooked arms and started dancing. When we finished we were breathless, and all of us laughed. I completely forgot this was a middle-aged woman I was dancing with.

"That was good!" she said. "Why, Tiny Lambert, where'd you learn to sing like that?"

For an instant the room faded away and I saw me and Willa up on the high porch in the swing, singing softly together.

"Just picked it up," I said to Mrs. Clevinger.

"Well, don't you ever lay it back down," she said, giggling. "And, Bobby Lynn, honey, you played just right—soft in the right places. I can't believe it. Can you do something else?"

Sure we could do something else, and we did something else and something else again while Mrs. Clevinger fried big slabs of pork and opened home-canned sauerkraut, and made corn bread. Then we sat down to eat in their cluttered kitchen.

"I have to drive up to Big Lick tonight to go to a wake," Mrs. Clevinger said. "I sure would like for you girls to go with me. I don't like driving in the dark by myself."

I didn't think I wanted to spend a Friday night sitting up with a corpse, but to my surprise, Bobby Lynn agreed.

"I've never been to a wake before," I said, somehow hoping that bit of information might save me, but I was wrong.

Next thing I knew, we were loaded into the Clevingers' Henry J, me in the front with Mrs. Clevinger, and Bobby Lynn in the back. We drove a long way up to Big Lick, almost to the West Virginia state line. We were cracking jokes and acting the fool all the way, and I never saw a grownup as much fun as Bobby Lynn's mama.

Then we turned up a gravel road that led to a great big farmhouse sitting in the crook of a holler. We put on some serious faces then and went in. I'm not sure what I expected a wake to be, but it wasn't what I found there.

The woman who died of old age was the mother of Mrs. Clevinger's lifelong friend Arbutus Shortridge. Her coffin was set up in the living room with flowers draped all over it, under it, around it, behind it. It put you in mind of a throne all decorated in finery, and the deceased was the queen presiding over the goings-on.

In every room there were clusters of people talking softly together, occasionally wiping away a tear as they told cute and touching stories about the star of the show, the deceased. Dead people are always remembered as wonderful.

Besides the heavy smell of flowers there was the smell of good food. On the kitchen table there was every kind of food you could ever want—stuff the neighbors had brought in. There was ham and fried chicken, freshly baked bread and biscuits, all kinds of vegetables and desserts—pumpkin pie and apple pie, pound cake and red velvet cake—and drinks. I think there were more drinks out in the barn, because the men would go out there looking very somber and sad, then come back in with a smile on their faces and smelling like something.

I discovered the object was to keep the dead body company all night and at the same time enjoy yourself as much as possible without making too much noise. Mrs. Clevinger found her friend Arbutus, and some other old friends she grew up with in Big Lick. So she settled down to talk to them while Bobby Lynn and I wandered around looking for some young people.

"Let's get some apple pie," Bobby Lynn whispered.

I followed her to the kitchen. A large-boned country girl perched on a stool by the table. She was pretty in a raw sort of way. She had freckles and brown pigtails, and a silly cock-eyed grin on her face. She tossed her pigtails around a lot and said, "Dead . . . dead . . ."

I poked Bobby Lynn and said with a giggle, "What's wrong with funny face?"

"Oh, that's Tilly Vanover," Bobby Lynn said. "She's not all there."

"What d'you mean?"

"Well, they say her daddy did you-know-what to her, and she lost something upstairs. She ain't been right since."

That bit of news made me feel so funny my knees buckled, and I had to sit down. Her daddy did you-know-what to her.

She lost something upstairs. She's not all there.

"What'sa matter with you?" Bobby Lynn said as she handed me a piece of pie on a saucer. "You see a ghost?"

"No. Nothing."

We took our pie into the dining room, where Arbutus' girl, Pearl, was sitting at a table with some other girls and a couple of boys. She introduced me to them, but for the moment I was so shaken I didn't hear or see anything. I ate my pie in silence, without looking up, as the young people chattered all around me in low voices.

Gradually I calmed down and silently vowed that I would not think of Tilly Vanover anymore.

There was a cute boy at the table who stared at me.

His name was Jesse Compton. He was medium in height and weight, with a blond crew cut and brown eyes. He was seventeen and a senior at Big Lick High School.

After a while I stared back at him.

The other boy was Patton Barber and he was ugly as a mud fence, but Bobby Lynn seemed to like him.

"Knock, knock," Bobby Lynn said in a whispery voice.

"Who's there?" we all said.

"Sam and Janet."

"Sam and Janet who?"

"Sam and Janet evening," she sang.

We laughed softly.

"I have one," Jesse said, and looked at me and winked.

My heart fluttered.

"Let's hear it," I said.

"Okay, you say 'Knock, knock,' " he said.

"Knock, knock," I said.

"Who's there?" he said.

There was silence for a minute, then we exploded.

A big fat woman came and looked in the door at us with her hands on her hips and a scowl on her face. We hung our heads in shame. As soon as she was gone we giggled into our hands.

"I got a Little Audrey joke," Patton Barber said.

"Let's hear it."

Jesse and I couldn't keep our eyes off each other. I had butterflies in my tummy. For about an hour we talked and told jokes as Jesse moved closer and closer to me.

Then a preacher started his sermon over the body. Tilly Vanover could be heard saying, "Dead . . . dead . . ." and somebody's false teeth were clicking as they ate. Otherwise only the preacher's voice could be heard throughout the house. If it hadn't been for Jesse staring at me I would have gone to sleep.

When the preacher finished, Mrs. Clevinger tiptoed in and whispered to me, "Arbutus wants somebody to sing 'Whispering Hope.' Will you do it?"

I fell back to Earth.

"In front of everybody?"

"Certainly. You can do it."

"I never did sing in front of people."

"Go on, Tiny," Bobby Lynn encouraged me. "I'll get you started."

My first reaction was to run. Then I thought, Why not? Why don't I do it real quick and not think about it, and I won't have a chance to get nervous?

Jesse was listening to our conversation. Wouldn't he be impressed? I jumped up so fast I knocked my chair over, and Jesse scrambled to pick it up for me. My heart was flying. Mrs. Clevinger and Bobby Lynn ushered me into the front room. Mrs. Clevinger said something to the people—I don't know what—then everybody was sitting there watching me and Bobby Lynn expectantly. I could feel my skirt fluttering against my legs where my knees were trembling. We stood by the casket. I looked at the body, then looked away quickly.

Bobby Lynn, with her perfect pitch, hummed a few bars for me to put me in the right key, and I began.

*Soft as the voice of an angel,*
*Breathing a lesson unheard,*
*Hope, with a gentle persuasion,*
*Whispers her comforting word.*
*Wait, till the darkness is over,*
*Wait, till the tempest is done,*
*Hope for the sunshine tomorrow,*
*After the shower is gone.*

I saw all the young people crowding into the doorway, watching and listening. Bobby Lynn edged away and stood by her mother. The relatives of the deceased started crying.

*Whispering Hope, oh, how welcome thy voice,*
*Making my heart in its sorrow rejoice.*

There were two more verses and I found myself relaxing. My voice rang out clear and true, right on key, even without a piano. I was proud of myself. When I finished, everybody was smiling at me through their tears, and hugging me. After all the compliments, Bobby Lynn and I went back in and sat down beside Patton and Jesse.

"That was real pretty, Tiny," he said.

"Thanks."

"Do you have a telephone, Tiny?"

"Yeah."

"Can I have your number?"

"Sure."

The clusters of mourners shifted around after midnight, and the young people resettled in the main room with the body. The hours started dragging, and a few people left. The chatter among us slowed down to a near stop. Jesse was beside me, but in spite of his presence, I started to nod around 3:00 a.m.

When I opened my eyes again, I sensed that some time had passed. Everybody in this room was asleep sitting up. Silence lay over the house like a blanket.

Slowly I got up and walked over to the coffin, and looked at the corpse. She was about eighty, I reckoned, all dressed up in silk and laid out in satin. Her white hair was streaked with yellow and slicked back over her pitiful shrunken skull. Her face was nearly as white as her hair, and wrinkled skin lay in folds around her mouth. Her shriveled hands were folded neatly across her waist and she held a single white carnation that was beginning to turn brown around the edges. I found myself watching for a heartbeat in the scrubby chest. What if she opened her eyes and looked at me?

She was once a girl, I thought, her body firm, her cheeks rosy, and her hair some soft, shiny color. She laughed and flirted with boys, and one of them fell in love with her and married her. Did they live happily ever after? And is this the end of ever after?

Suddenly I heard someone breathing behind me, and I nearly jumped out of my skin.

I turned to face Tilly Vanover.

"Dead . . . dead . . ." she said.

She was still standing there a few moments later when I left with Bobby Lynn and her mother. I felt very sorry for her.

On the way back to Black Gap, Bobby Lynn slept

in the back seat. Mrs. Clevinger was tired and didn't say a word. But my mind was busy.

The first frost of the winter had settled during the night. Not a soul was astir in Black Gap, and not a car moving. The little town was sleeping snugly in its pocket against the mountain. I watched the sun rise over the golden Appalachians and everything was sparkling like diamonds in the frost.

"I *survived!*" I was thinking. "And I am fully alive! I am alive and this is a magic moment because I *know* I am alive. I am alive and I am sixteen, and it is dawn on a Saturday morning in October in 1958. I am in a Henry J riding up Main Street in Black Gap, Virginia, U.S.A., North America, Earth . . ."

And as quickly as that, the moment was gone.

# EIGHTEEN

⚐ I was dead asleep in the middle of the afternoon when Beau opened my door and hollered, "Git up, Tiny! There's a boy on the phone for you."

I swung my feet to the floor, and shook my head.

A boy? Jesse!

I stumbled down the stairs to the phone in the hall.

"Hello."

"Hello, Tiny? This is Jesse."

He did! He called! He said he would call and he did!

"Who?" I said.

"Jesse Compton. You remember, we met last night at Big Lick."

"Oh, hey, Jesse. What a surprise!"

"Hope I'm not interrupting anything."

"No, I was just . . . doing some stuff. Nothing special."

"Well, I wondered if maybe we could go to a show tonight in Black Gap."

"I guess so. What's playing?"

"I don't know."

"That's okay."

"You'll go?"

"I gotta ask Mama."

"You want me to hang on while you ask her?"

"That's okay. She'll say yes."

"Good. Seven-thirty?"

"That's okay."

"One more thing."

"Yeah?"

"Where do you live?"

"Oh, Ruby Valley. You know where that is?"

"I think so."

So we spent the next five minutes going over the route to my house; then we hung up.

I had a date. My first date. And he was real cute. He had his driver's license. He was smart. He played football.

I took a deep breath and went into the kitchen, where Mama and Vern were eating something at the table.

"Can I go out tonight, Mama?"

"Where to?"

"To a show."

"Who with?"

"Just a boy."

Both their heads shot up.

"What boy?" they said together.

"I met him last night."

"What's his name?" Vern said.

I ignored him.

"He has a blond crew cut, Mama."

"Well, who is he?" she said.

"Jesse Compton."

"We don't know no Comptons."

"He's from Big Lick."

Mama and Vern looked at each other.

"Well, what's he like?" she said.

"He's real cute."

"Who's his daddy?" Vern said, and I ignored him again.

"Mrs. Clevinger told me she grew up with his mama," I said.

"Who's his daddy?" Vern repeated.

"I dunno," I mumbled.

"Well, is he gonna come in the house and meet us like a gentleman," Mama said, "or is he gonna sit outside and blow his horn?"

"Oh, Mama," I said, sighing. "You know he'll come in!"

They were both quiet.

"You'll like him, Mama," I said.

"Mmmmmmmm . . ." was all she said.

I went back to my room quickly, hoping they would say no more.

About six o'clock I took a bath; thirty minutes later I was back in my room wrapped up in my robe when Vern suddenly pushed open my door and stuck his old bald head in. He had a strange expression on his face.

"What d'you want?" I said, pulling my robe tightly around me.

"I just want to tell you, you better behave yourself tonight with that boy."

My volcano started to spew toward the top.

"If you don't get out of my room right now," I hissed at him, "I will scream for Mama."

"This is not *your* room!" he hissed back. "I paid for everything in this house, and that includes that damn dawg!"

He backed out and closed the door without another word.

I had to sit down to still my trembling. That fat old pig was jealous of Jesse. I clenched my fists in determination. I would *not* let him spoil my date. I *would* have a good time. I sat there pulling myself back together.

I wore my blue-and-green-plaid skirt, my blue sweater with matching cardigan, loafers, and blue knee socks. I put my hair up in a high ponytail and taped spit curls around my face. I put on just enough lipstick, and curled my eyelashes. I would wear my band letter jacket.

Well, I thought, as I stood in front of the mirror and remembered what Aunt Evie told me that day about saying nice things to myself. You look good, Tiny Lambert! You look pretty, and Jesse Compton is going to fall madly in love with you this night. How can he resist?

Then I practiced smiling and greeting him at the door.

"Well, hi, Jesse! I guess you found me."

No.

"Jesse! Is it seven-thirty already?"

No.

"Hi there! Come in and meet my mama."

Would Vern say something stupid to Jesse? If he said anything at all it would be stupid. Maybe he would just be quiet.

I took the tape off my spit curls, picked up my pocketbook, and went down to the living room, where I found Mama, Vern, and all the kids watching television. I was nervous.

I sat down between Mama and Luther.

> *Pamper, Pamper, new shampoo*
> *Gentle as a lamb, so right for you!*
> *Gentle as a lamb?*
> *Yes, ma'am!*
> *Pamper, Pamper, new shampoo.*

Would I have to introduce him to everybody?

"You look pretty, Tiny," Mama interrupted my thoughts. "Your hair shines just like you been using Pamper."

"Where you goin' to?" Phyllis demanded to know.

She was curled up beside Vern on the other couch with her bare cold feet pushed up under him.

I didn't answer her.

"Mama, where's Tiny goin' to?" she persisted.

"Y'all be quiet!" Beau shouted.

He was trying to watch *Have Gun Will Travel*.

"Tiny's got a date," Vern announced just because he knew I didn't want a lot of attention.

I could have killed him.

"A date?"

"Tiny's got a date?"

"Who with?"

"Where you goin' to?"

I got up and marched out of the room into the kitchen. Phyllis followed me.

"Who is he, Tiny?"

"Why don't you put your shoes on?" I screamed at her.

She looked down at her dirty, bare feet dumbly.

"Sometimes y'all act like a bunch of hillbillies!" I sputtered.

"Who is he, Tiny?"

I just knew Jesse would come now while everybody was asking a lot of dumb questions. They would gawk at him and giggle and act stupid. I was so nervous I couldn't sit down. I started pacing the kitchen floor.

"Who is he, Tiny?" Phyllis said for the third time.

"You don't know him."

"What's his name?"

"Jesse."

"That's a girl's name."

"It is not, and don't you go out there and say something stupid like that to him."

"What about Jessie Deal and Jessie Lou Looney?" she went on. "They're girls."

"And what about Jesse James?" I said. "He's a boy."

"Who's Jesse James?"

Lordy.

"Just leave me alone, Phyllis."

"What does he look like?"

"He's real cute."

"Is he tall?"

"Not real."

"Short?"

"No, medium."

"Dark hair or blond?"

Somebody knocked on the front door, and my heart jumped. God, don't let Vern go to the door. But I should be so lucky. Phyllis, Luther, and Beau scrambled all over each other and fell out the door in a pile, while Nessie started barking and going around in circles. I closed my eyes.

"Does Tiny Lambert live here?" I heard Jesse's voice.

"Tiny!" they all yelled for me, but I was right there by then.

"Hi, Jesse, come in and meet everybody," I said, feeling my face flame.

Three pairs of blue eyes stared at him.

"Well, you've met these three," I said. "Beau, Luther, and Phyllis."

Nessie barked and everybody laughed.

"Oh yes, and that's Nessie, short for Tennessee," I said, loosening up.

I closed the door as Jesse stepped inside. He had on his football jacket—maroon and white.

Mama and Vern stared as much as the kids. I introduced them.

Mama said, "Hey, Jesse."

But Vern sat in silence. I wanted to get away from him as soon as possible.

"Where you goin' to?" Phyllis said.

"To a show, I reckon?" Jesse said and looked at me.

"I reckon," I said.

"Indoors or out?" Vern said.

Him and his dirty mind.

But Jesse didn't understand.

"What?"

"You goin' to a drive-in show?" Vern said.

"It's almost November, Vern," I said sharply. "The drive-in closed a month ago."

I turned to Jesse quickly. "Ready to go?"

"Yeah."

I grabbed my school band jacket and my pocket-book.

"Glad I met y'all," Jesse said.

"Yeah, nice to meet you, too, Jesse," Mama said. "Now, Tiny, you remember to be back here by eleven."

We were out the door and I breathed a sigh of relief. We looked at each other and grinned as we went down the tall steps.

"Hi," I said.

"Hi, yourself."

That was nice.

The air was clean and crisp and the sky perfectly velvet blue, with a little sliver of moon rocking on a mountaintop.

"You look pretty," he said, and I smiled up at him.

He had a brown-and-white '57 Chevy, absolutely spotless. I loved it. He opened the door for me and I slid in. I could feel the kids all staring at us from the front window. Well, let 'em stare. He came around to the driver's side, got in, and started the car. He had automatic transmission.

"Nice car, Jesse."

"It's my daddy's, but I drive it all the time. He lets me as long as I take good care of it, and I do."

We backed down to the road and headed toward the highway. We talked about the football season that ended last week. Black Gap and Big Lick both had winning seasons. We usually beat Big Lick, but this year they beat us.

"You stomped us," I said. "That was a good game."

"They had us right there till the last quarter. Say, I remember the band. Y'all were real good. Didn't you play 'Dixie'?"

"Yeah."

"And 'His Truth Is Marching On'?"

"Yeah, 'Battle Hymn of the Republic.' "

He was groping around for my hand and I helped him find it.

"Come on over closer," he said, and I slid across the wide seat beside him.

"I thought about you all day," he said. "I couldn't sleep even after staying up all night."

"I thought about you, too."

"Did you want me to call?"

"Sure I did."

Then we glanced at each other and smiled.

It was cold and Jesse turned on the heat. Shortly we were cruising down Main Street, and ready for a Saturday-night date in Black Gap.

The movie was at the Regal. There was another theater in town, but nobody ever went there on a Saturday. It was understood that the Regal was the only place to be. The movie was something with Jane Powell or Dick Powell—I don't remember which one. We bought snacks, then went up to the balcony. Every popular person I knew was there. They hollered hey to me. Some of them knew Jesse and hollered at him, too. I was proud to be seen with him.

It was dim up there and the air was heavy with that theater smell—popcorn and bodies—and the floor was sticky and grungy with thousands of pops and food of all the Saturday nights before still clinging. We found seats by the railing and settled down with all our stuff.

Before the cartoon was over I heard my name called, and there was Rosemary and Roy. We made a lot of commotion as they settled in beside us, and I introduced everybody. Rosemary poked me and whispered, "He's cute!"

The cartoon ended and the newsreel came on. Jesse took my hand and we snuggled shoulder to shoulder. By the time the movie ended, our palms were stuck together with sweat.

"Y'all come go with us to the CAR-feteria," Rosemary said. "Everybody'll be there."

"Why don't y'all come with us?" Jesse said.

Yeah, I was thinking, that would be better because I wanted to be seen with Jesse in his Chevy.

Roy and Rosemary agreed.

You could always tell when the Regal let out on Saturday night because a solid line of cars streamed down Main Street to the drive-in restaurant. The CAR-feteria was just out of town at a wide place in the road so there was plenty of parking space and room to cruise in and out among the cars. And that's what everybody spent a lot of time doing on Saturday night. It was stroll-and-perch time in cars.

We ordered hot dogs—no onions—and cherry Cokes. Roy ordered a big dill pickle just to be different.

Then there was Connie Collins right beside us with one of the Owens boys in a new Lincoln with a Continental kit. And she had on a black mouton jacket. Did she always have to outdo everybody in everything?

"Hey, Connie!" Rosemary called to her sweetly.

Connie flashed a big toothy grin. We waved at her. She started looking at Jesse and he started looking at her like they never saw the opposite sex before.

"I can't stand that girl," Rosemary and I said together, but still smiling.

"What girl?" Jesse said.

"Connie Collins," Roy said. "The blonde in the Lincoln."

"Oh," Jesse said. "I was just admiring the Continental kit."

"Sure you were!" we teased him.

"I really was," he said. "The prettiest girls here tonight are in my car!"

And he squeezed my hand.

Our hot dogs came, and I don't remember if mine was good or not. It didn't matter. We were having fun, and nothing could spoil it. Roy passed around that silly pickle and made everybody take a bite. We laughed till we hurt.

Later, Jesse drove me home and we were quiet all the way. I was thinking, I never want this night to end. I'm going to remember it all—the balcony and

Roy and Rosemary, and the CAR-feteria and that pickle and how everything smelled and how the Chevy chrome sparkled in the lights, and how Jesse said I was pretty and held my hand. And I'm going to remember everything he said and write it all down when I get home. Because this is the beginning of happily ever after, and I don't want to forget any of it.

We sat in the Chevy on the little dirt road going up the hill to my house and looked at the night and still said nothing. It must have been about five minutes till eleven. All the lights in my house were out except for the living room, where I knew Mama was watching the last few minutes of television before it signed off; and the front porch light was on, of course. Vern, no doubt, saw to that.

"I have to go in," I said at last.

Jesse got out and came over to my side and helped me out like they do in the movies. Then he put his arm around me and we went up the tall steps like that. On the top step right under the porch light he kissed me.

"Call you tomorrow," he whispered.

And he left.

I floated into the house.

Whee . . . eee . . .

# NINETEEN

Jesse called the next day and we went for a ride up the river. I heard from him on Monday, Tuesday, and the rest of the week, but it was Friday before I saw him again. By that time I couldn't bring up his face in my mind's eye, but when he came to the door Friday night, it all rushed back to me: his special smell, the way he looked at me, this habit he had of cocking his head to the side when he teased me.

That night we went to the sock hop in the school gym, sponsored by the Band Parents. I wore my black slacks and my white Banlon cardigan buttoned up the back. It was the style. Jesse wore corduroy. We were together most of the weekend, and it whirled by breathlessly. I couldn't write it all down or remember it. I wanted everything to slow down so I could hold on to it a little longer and think about it while it was happening. But there was no time for holding or thinking, and I learned as the weeks went by to go with the moment, to love it better than any other moment, then let it go, and hurry to the next one.

Sometimes we sat in his car and kissed till our lips were numb and we were breathless. Then Jesse would say, "I wish we were married."

And I would say, "Me too."

But we didn't do a thing. Just talked about it, and the shining future that spread out before us. Jesse was planning to work for his daddy in his welding shop, and someday we were going to get married. We would live with his folks until we could afford to build our dream house. Then we would have babies . . . and they would grow up and have babies . . . and we would be grandparents . . . then . . . ?

Sometimes when we were kissing in Jesse's car in the driveway, I would see Vern looking out the window. I was overwhelmed with shame, and I wished he would just drop dead and be out of my life. I vowed never, never to tell anybody—never. I would die if Jesse found out what Vern did to me. It would be the awfulest thing that ever was if Jesse found out.

Then I tried to forget it and wipe it out of my mind. But I woke up in a panic in the night two or three times. I was dreaming, but I couldn't remember what.

"I will forget," I said to myself. "I will never tell— ever. And I will forget about it. Then it will be like it never did happen."

At Christmas, Jesse gave me his class ring, and I wore it on a chain around my neck. That meant we were going steady. About that time, Mama decided to act like a real mama and give me a good talking-to. It was that old "all boys are after one thing" talk. I had heard it a thousand times from every woman I knew. I acted like I was taking everything in, and agreeing. All the time I was thinking about Mama and Ernest Bevins up on Ruby Mountain getting me. In the end she made me promise not to "do anything" I would regret, and not to be alone with Jesse so much, because it bothered Vern. He was real worried, she said, about me getting in trouble. Well, she could have gone all day without saying that. It did nothing but make me mad.

"It's none of his business!" I snapped.

"It most certainly is his business," Mama said. "He don't want another mouth to feed around here any more than I do."

I sighed heavily and said, "Mama, give me credit for some sense. I'm not going to get in trouble."

"No girl plans to get in trouble," she went on. "I know I didn't. It just happened."

So she had done her duty.

When I wasn't in school or with Jesse, I was with Aunt Evie. She was as eager as a girl herself to hear all about me and Jesse. I could talk about him all I wanted, and she was all ears. She giggled and dreamed with me, and helped me make plans.

Although Bobby Lynn was dating Cecil a lot, they weren't serious. They both dated other people, but Rosemary and Roy were thick as molasses. They planned to get married the day after graduation. Roy was going to go into the mines with his daddy and brothers.

It was about that time, early in 1959, that Mama got real interested in visiting sick people in the hospital, with Dixie. They went about once or twice a week, and the kids went along to ride on the elevator. It was the only one in town, and they would ride it up and down, up and down, till somebody made them stop. When everybody was going to be gone after school I would hurry into the house, change clothes, get something to eat, and go up to Aunt Evie's before Vern got home from work. I stayed with her until Mama came home. Then one afternoon in mid-March, when I got off the bus I saw the pickup parked in its usual spot. I knew Mama and the kids were gone, and I couldn't figure out why Vern was home so early, but I decided to go straight up to Aunt Evie's. I was rounding the corner of the house where the kitchen window was open a bit when I heard a voice from inside. He meant for me to hear.

"Look, Nessie, Tiny's going up the hill to Aunt Evie's. She don't care if you get hurt or not."

I stood still. Would he really hurt Nessie? I had visions of him hitting her with his belt or kicking her, or . . . Slowly I eased into the kitchen, but he wasn't there anymore. For a moment I stood in silence.

Then I called, "Nessie! Come here, Nessie!"

But she did not come. I thought, He must be holding her, or she would come to me. Slowly I walked to the living-room door. Vern was watching television and clutching Nessie's collar.

"Come on in, Tiny," he said. "I don't want you to be afraid of me."

"I ain't afraid. Just let Nessie go."

"Come on over here and sit beside me. I won't lay a hand on you."

"Just let Nessie go."

"Come here and I will."

I felt safe beside the front door. If I went farther in, I might not be able to get back to the door.

"Vern, if you'll let Nessie go, I'll come in and sit by you."

"Come on, now. Come on over here and talk to me. I don't like you being scared of me."

"Let me stand here."

"Come on. I won't lay a hand on you. Word of honor."

Slowly I walked in and sat on the edge of the couch. I could smell bourbon. Nessie started straining for me and Vern turned her loose. I started petting her and eyeing the door.

"I never meant to make you mad," Vern said seriously, and for a minute I thought he was going to apologize. "I could have been a lot nicer."

I didn't say anything. I would give him a minute, then I would bolt.

"You know I love you, Tiny. That's the only reason I done it. Don't you believe me?"

I didn't trust my voice, and I felt like throwing up.

Silence fell between us. I could hear him wheezing as he breathed. On television Jack Bailey was saying, "Would you like to be Queen for a Day?"

"Is it better with Jesse?" Vern said.

I stood up and took Nessie's collar.

"Just hold on," Vern said, grabbing my wrist.

His grip was steel.

"Vern . . . please."

Panic was just beneath the surface.

And then the miracle happened. There was a knock at the front door and I heard Cecil's voice.

"Hey, Tiny! You home?"

"Come on in, Cecil!" I hollered real loud. "I'm here in the living room."

Vern let go of me as Cecil entered the hallway. I walked unsteadily toward the living-room door as Cecil entered the room.

"Hey, Tiny."

"Hey, Cecil."

He looked from me to Vern.

"Bobby Lynn just called me about the talent show . . . Is something wrong?"

"No. Let's go for a walk. Come on, Nessie! Let's go, girl."

Vern sat in silence as we left with Cecil.

"What's going on?" Cecil said when we were walking down the hill.

"What d'you mean?"

"You look funny."

Cecil stopped walking and peered down at me with his brow all wrinkled up. It struck me at that moment how handsome he was silhouetted against the sky like that. When did Cecil grow up to be so good-looking?

"What's going on?" he repeated.

"Nothing."

He didn't persist, and I was glad.

"Let's just walk up the road for a piece," I said. "Okay?"

"Sure."

We set off walking up the dirt road, kicking rocks as we went. The air smelled good, but there was a wind and I shivered. Cecil kept looking at me with a puzzled expression on his face. He was the one who should be shivering, I thought. I still had on my band jacket, but he was in his shirt sleeves.

"I'm sorry, Cecil. I didn't even notice, but I bet you're cold."

"Not a bit."

"What about the talent show?" I said.

"They moved it back to April because it's got to be such a big thing, they don't want it too close to the beauty contest in May."

"That's good."

"Bobby Lynn wanted me to talk to you. She thinks you have the best chance of winning. She wants to play piano for you."

Maybe I would enter that talent show and win this year. That's what I would do.

"Is Bobby Lynn going to yodel?"

"No, she's not eligible to enter again. She wants you to win. So do I."

"Thanks, Cecil."

"The jewelry store is giving a seventeen-jewel Elgin, and the dime store is giving a gift certificate. And the Miner's Diner is giving a free dinner for four."

We glanced at each other.

"So if you win, you can pick out four people you don't like and send 'em over there to eat."

We laughed.

"Now, are you going to tell me what's wrong?"

"Nothing's wrong, Cecil."

"Okay, if you say so."

"I'm going to do it, Cecil. I mean I'm going to enter the talent contest."

"Good. Now Bobby Lynn will get off my back."

I stayed with Cecil until Mama and the kids came home near dark, and he didn't ask me any more questions.

Next day I entered the talent contest, and Bobby Lynn and I set about practicing in earnest. Vern said very little to me after that day, which was fine with me, and I said nothing to him at all, which was usual. Still he stared at me all the time. I could feel his eyes on me when I was watching the television or washing dishes. Sometimes when I was outside I saw him standing looking out the window. He made my skin crawl.

Every morning on the radio they announced what prizes had been added to the pool for the winner of the talent show. The A & P chipped in a big gift certificate, and the Style Shoppe gave fifty dollars' worth of clothes. The Ford dealership gave a set of tires, the department store a set of luggage, the appliance store a radio, and on and on.

There was a piano in the band room, and that's where Bobby Lynn and I practiced every day at lunchtime, and that's where I finally made an impression on Mr. Gillespie. The first time he heard me singing, he stopped whatever it was he was doing at his desk and came around and stood by the piano and listened. He made me so nervous I forgot the words. After he told me how good I was, he had me going up and down the scales to find my range, and all kinds of technical stuff like that.

"We have to practice," Bobby Lynn told him.

"Oh, sure," he said. "But later, Tiny, after the talent show, I want you to come in and let me help you with your breathing."

I was thinking I knew how to breathe just fine.

"And I'd like to talk to both of you about this school down in North Carolina."

That again. He was always going on about that college where his wife had gone.

So Bobby Lynn and I decided on a fast song, "Lipstick on Your Collar," and a slow one, "Over the Rainbow." Bobby Lynn was almost as excited as I was, and when Jesse and I double-dated with her and Cecil on Saturday night, all she could talk about was the talent show and how she knew I was going to win. I started feeling like I had to win.

"If she sings anywhere near as good as she did the night I met her, she'll win," Jesse said. "Won't you, Pea Blossom?"

Pea Blossom? Love has no sense.

Connie Collins looked better and better when I saw her practicing after school sometimes. Nobody could deny she was a good dancer—too good. Fear started gnawing at me. What if she beat me?

Bobby Lynn helped me pick out the prettiest dress I ever had, and it cost the most, too. It was royal blue, elbow-length sleeves, slightly off the shoulders, fitting me snugly to right below the knee.

And the next thing I knew, it was the big night. I was in the wings peeping out at the crowd through the curtains. There was Mama and Phyllis right on the front row with Roy and Rosemary, Cecil and Jesse.

As I watched Willard Newberry playing his guitar and struggling through "Ghost Riders in the Sky," I thought it was funny I didn't feel anything at all— no excitement or nervousness or any other emotion. Maybe I was in shock. Then Willard's number was over and I stepped out on the stage and looked at the sea of waiting, expectant faces. Hundreds of eyes were on me, hundreds of ears tuned into my frequency, hundreds of brains clicking into the fact that Tiny Lambert was on stage and fixing to sing. Hundreds of minds were asking themselves, "Can Tiny Lambert sing?" "Is Tiny Lambert going to make a big fool of herself?"

And a great, cold monster of fear clutched me right around the middle so hard it like to have knocked the breath out of me, and it began to play my heart like a kettle drum.

The lights went down. A deathly stillness settled over the auditorium, and Bobby Lynn played a terrifyingly short introduction to "Over the Rainbow." I was frozen. She played it again.

I opened my mouth and my lips stuck to my teeth, as the usual moisture there had totally evaporated. I heard this little bitty squeak come out of my throat.

"Some . . . where . . ."

That was all.

Bobby Lynn tried again with the introduction.

"Some . . . where . . ." the tiny voice squeaked again.

Was it hours and hours that I stood there trying to move on to the word "over"? Or was it only a minute before some kind soul mercifully rang down the curtain? I left the stage in humiliation.

Connie Collins won the talent contest that year.

# TWENTY

⚰ "I think you ought to cut it about an inch," Rosemary was saying to me about my hair.

We were lying in the daisies up on Ruby Mountain
by the natural spring. It was a day . . . well, it was the
most heavenly Sunday in spring you can imagine.

"And curl it."

"What about the ponytail? Am I too old for a
ponytail?"

"You will be in two weeks."

In two weeks I would be seventeen.

"But for now?" I said.

"You're still sweet sixteen!" she said, laughing.

It was two weeks after the disaster. I wouldn't let
anyone, including myself, speak of "that night."

"I'll get it cut when I am officially a senior, and not wear a ponytail anymore," I declared.

Rosemary was the first girl of our crowd to get her driver's license. That day she had driven her daddy's pickup, and we couldn't think of anyplace to go, so I decided to show her Ruby Mountain.

We were sitting by the spring and I was dipping my fingers in the cold, cold water and flicking poor Nessie in the face. She jumped up, shook her head, and lay back down again.

"Wouldn't you think she'd move to another spot?" Rosemary said.

"You'd think so," I agreed.

It was the first day I could remember with just me and Rosemary. There was always somebody else around us.

"She ain't too bright," I said, and flicked Nessie again.

That time she got up and walked away from me about ten feet, where she lay down in the sunshine. We laughed. We were wearing our shorts and halters, trying to get some sun.

"Well, how many months, weeks, hours until the wedding day, Rosemary?"

Rosemary brushed away a stray strand of dark hair from her face and mumbled, "I dunno. I lost count."

"What'sa matter, Rosemary?"

"Nothing."

"You still plan to marry Roy, don't you?"

"Oh, sure! We love each other. What else would we do?"

"Yeah, what else?" I said.

"Well, there's college," Rosemary said.

I wasn't sure I heard her right.

"Come again?"

"Well, Mr. Gillespie keeps talking about that school in North Carolina where they teach a lot of music. And sometimes . . ."

She paused and looked out at the distant hills.

"Sometimes I think maybe—just maybe, mind you—I might like to go to college—even for a year— you know, just to see what it's like."

"College?"

"Yeah, college. You know—where people go to get educated."

"Sure, I know what college is. The town kids go to college."

"Does that mean we can't go, Tiny, because we're not town kids?"

"No."

Rosemary's parents had the store and they could probably afford to send her to school if they wanted to. But her family was like mine. None of them ever went to college.

"What for?" I said.

"What d'you mean, what for? To get an education, that's what for."

"Then what?"

"I would marry Roy."

"Oh."

"I know it's crazy." Rosemary laughed at herself. "I really don't want to go. I just like to think about it." She rolled over on her back and gazed up at the sky.

College? I was thinking. Well, that's one I never

considered before, because I knew it wasn't one of my choices. I always knew I would finish high school and get married and have babies, because that's what girls do. And now that I was in love with Jesse, I knew that's what I wanted.

"What would you study?" I said.

"Music," she replied promptly. "And if I finished, it would be nice to have a job like Mr. Gillespie's. It would be fun."

"Yeah, it would be. Then why don't you do it, Rosemary?"

"Oh, I'm just talking, Tiny. I want to marry Roy. I don't think he can wait much longer for . . . you know."

We giggled.

"I want to get married, Rosemary," I said. "It's all I've ever wanted. I just know I'm going to be happy with Jesse."

"It's nice here with you and without anybody else around," she said. "I don't know when me and Roy have spent a Sunday apart."

"Where is Roy, anyway?"

"He's helping his daddy overhaul an engine or something. Where's Jesse?"

"He took his mama to Honaker to see her relations."

"Why didn't you go, Tiny?"

I had been wondering that myself.

"He didn't ask me to go. That seems funny, don't it?"

"You oughta be glad he didn't. Nothing's more boring than sitting around listening to relations talking about other relations, and you don't know any of them."

"I know. I'm glad you came by. This is fun."

I lay back on the grass, closed my eyes, and let the sun fall on my face and throat. It was like a caress, soft and warm. I loved this place above all others.

"I wish I had me a car," Rosemary said. "One of my very own."

"Me too. Did you know Mrs. Clevinger is trying to sell the Henry J?"

"No, is she?"

"Yeah, she has her eye on a '57 Plymouth Fury, two-toned burgundy and white."

"How much does she want for the Henry J?" Rosemary said.

"Three hundred."

"That's not much, but Daddy would never let me have it."

"Why don't we . . . ?" I sat up quickly as an idea took root. "We could buy it together, you, me, and Bobby Lynn. I know she'd like that."

"I don't have a hundred, Tiny, do you?"

"Not now. But the strawberries are ready to ripen again. I'll have at least a hundred in a few weeks."

Rosemary lit up.

"Can I help pick?"

"Sure! There's enough for everybody. Bobby Lynn, too. There's our three hundred."

"Tiny, you are a genius! Can we really make that much on strawberries?"

"We can make as much as we have time to make," I said. "We have to go to school."

"Then we'll come up here every day after school and every weekend."

Suddenly Rosemary got a funny look on her face as she turned toward the cabin.

"What's it like in there?" she said.

"In the cabin? Oh, it's okay. It's small."

"Furniture?"

"Yeah, just like Grandpa left it."

"Beds?"

"Yeah, two. What are you thinking?"

"We could come up here and stay through strawberry season!"

"You mean it, don't you?" I said.

"I do. I mean it. Gosh, think of the fun we could have—just the three of us."

"But what about school?"

"Oh, we'll go to school. Daddy can drive the Studebaker and I'll borrow his truck. He'll let me have it—to get up here and to school."

"And we could bring food from home," I said. "And here's our water. But there's no electricity, Rosemary. No lights."

"We don't need lights. We'll be too tired to stay up after dark anyway."

"Let's do it!"

We stood up and hugged each other and squealed.

Then we went into the cabin. Everything we needed was there to live for a few weeks. A coal stove for cooking, beds, dishes, pots and pans, odds and ends of furniture, and an outdoor toilet. We drove back down the mountain in high spirits. First step was to ask Mama. She was getting ready to go to the hospital and wasn't very interested in anything else.

"Reckon so," was all she said as she glanced out the window to look for Dixie's car.

Vern said, "As long as there ain't no boys up there after dark."

I groaned inside, and didn't look at him.

"Did you hear me, girlie?" he said.

"I heard."

"No boys after dark," he repeated.

I was wondering how he was going to know if we had boys up there after dark or not.

"I'll be checking up on you," he said like he was reading my mind. "And if I ever catch a boy with you after dark, it's all over."

Rosemary and I looked at each other and shrugged. After all, the object was to pick as many strawberries as possible.

"Fine with me," she said.

"Yeah," I said. "Me too."

Next we called Rosemary's mama, who asked a lot of questions, but she finally said yes.

Then we called Bobby Lynn, who was very excited, and of course Mrs. Clevinger said, "Yes! Yes! Yes!" because she wanted to sell us the Henry J.

So that's how it happened that when the first strawberry on Ruby Mountain turned red, Rosemary, Bobby Lynn, and I were standing there looking at it. We pounced upon it and were off and running.

To tell the truth, the first week we didn't get many berries at all. They weren't quite ready, but we sure had a good time. After we picked what berries were ripe in the afternoons after school, we took them down to Mama, and she and the kids went out selling just before dark. We went back up on Ruby Mountain and cooked hot dogs mostly, or beans and taters. Sometimes we had sandwiches and pop.

By Saturday afternoon of that first week we ran out of anything to do and we got bored. Only I knew what was coming the next week and the next. We sure wouldn't have time to get bored when the strawberries really came on thick.

But that day I suggested we cook up some hamburgers for the fellers who were coming up there directly. Rosemary went down to the company store, while Bobby Lynn and I cleaned up the cabin and fixed the fire outside. Nessie knew something exciting was coming about and she got under our feet and barked at us like she was trying to talk. So I talked to her and told her what was happening.

Rosemary came back and we started frying hamburgers, and baking taters in the fire. It was beginning to smell good when Jesse and Roy arrived with Cecil in Cecil's daddy's truck. Cecil backed the truck up to the outside fire and turned on the radio.

"So fine, yeah!" the radio blared out. Jesse grabbed me around the waist, and we started dancing around the fire as free as Indians.

"My baby's so doggone fine," Jesse sang with the radio, but he couldn't carry a tune in a bucket. We laughed hard.

Then Roy and Rosemary, Cecil and Bobby Lynn all started dancing, too.

"She sends those chills up and down my spine."

We were whirling around the fire, and all over the mountaintop, while Nessie barked at our feet.

"Oh . . . oh . . . yeah . . . So fine."

Afterward we sat on the ground and ate hamburgers hot off the fire, and drank pop. We could have stayed together for hours, but you could see the sun tapping a distant mountaintop and WBGV Radio in Black Gap was signing off with "Come home, come home, it's supper time," as it did every day.

"Vern says y'all have to be gone by dark," I said.

"Yeah, I know," Jesse said.

Then he took my hand and whispered, "Let's go for a walk."

We walked away from the others and around to the other side of the cabin, where the weeping willow was softly sweeping.

"Let's crawl up under the willow," Jesse said.

So we did.

Well, it was nice—cool and dark and private under there. We lay on the ground and started kissing. Pretty soon I had to push him away as I was always doing these days.

"What'sa matter, Tiny?"

"Stop."

"I don't want to stop, and I don't want to wait no more."

"We've talked about this before, Jesse."

"Yeah, but it's time to reconsider."

"I don't know, Jesse . . ."

"We can do what we want if we're careful, Tiny."

"What d'you mean?"

"Just that. There are ways to keep from getting pregnant."

"So they say."

"Well, I can't wait, Tiny. Can you honestly say it's easy for you?"

"No, it ain't easy, Jesse."

"There! Will you think about it?"

"Well . . ."

"Promise me you'll think about it."

"I promise."

We crawled out from under the willow and joined the others. Shortly thereafter Vern came driving up the mountain with Phyllis beside him and Beau and Luther in the back. He parked the truck a ways from the cabin and watched us. The boys took the hint. Darkness was coming anyway. They left, and then Vern left, too.

# TWENTY-ONE

≱ Afterward Bobby Lynn, Rosemary, and I built up the fire and started singing "On Top of Old Smokey"—all forty verses.

It was a crystal-clear night with millions of stars all around us. The moon was full to bustin', and so round and bright it seemed like you could walk out to the edge of the mountaintop and reach right up and grab it in your arms.

Then Rosemary brought out a pack of Lucky Strikes and we started puffing like we smoked cigarettes regular. But it was really our first smoke unless you count the corn silks as kids.

"What brought this on, Rosemary?" Bobby Lynn said. "How come you got cigarettes?"

"Oh . . . Roy!" Rosemary sputtered. "He said the other day that no wife of his was ever going to smoke cigarettes. I never wanted to smoke till he said that. So today at the store I felt like buying a pack."

"You're strange, Rosemary Layne," I said. "You know that? You're strange."

She grinned, and puffed.

We practiced holding the cigarette just right, and flashing it around for dramatic effect as we talked. It wasn't bad if you pulled the smoke in just a little bit, and blew it out real fast before you could taste it.

Then Rosemary said, "I have a suggestion."

We watched her light up a second cigarette.

"Who wants to play One Question?"

We were silent.

One Question was more a test of loyalty than a game. Only the best of friends played it, and we had never played it before. Everybody must want to play, and everybody must swear never to tell the answer to the One Question.

What you did was ask the One Question you always wanted to ask your friend, but you didn't because it was too personal. And when it came your turn to answer, you had to tell the truth. It was no telling what they might ask. Still I said, "Okay, I'll play."

"Me too," Bobby Lynn said.

So we got in a huddle and drew straws. Bobby Lynn lost, so she would get the One Question first. Rosemary and I walked away from her and discussed what we wanted to ask. We had to agree, and we had to word the question so she couldn't answer with a simple yes or no. Then we walked back to the fire and sat down one on either side of her. She seemed to be holding her breath.

"This is our One Question for you, Bobby Lynn," Rosemary said. "What happened between your mama and daddy?"

All the air went out of Bobby Lynn, and she drooped.

"They were fighting all the time," she said quickly as if she had rehearsed her answer. "And she wanted him to leave. So they are getting a divorce. I haven't seen him in months, and I miss him."

She seemed real sad and I was almost sorry we had asked her.

"She said the feeling was gone," Bobby Lynn went on almost like she was talking to herself or thinking out loud. "And he said—I'll never forget it—he said, 'Love is more than a feeling.' "

Nobody said anything for a while.

Bobby Lynn said it again, "Love is more than a feeling."

Then silence.

We couldn't ask anything else, and she seemed to be finished.

"Okay, Tiny," Rosemary said. "Your turn."

The two of them got up and walked into the shadows. I couldn't imagine what they would ask me, but I suddenly thought of Vern, and my blood ran cold. Could they possibly suspect? How could they know? No, it wasn't possible. Still I couldn't shake the paralyzing fear that somehow they would word their question so that I would have to tell. I would lie, no matter what. I would never tell.

They came back and I was afraid they would see how scared I was.

"Who is your daddy?" Bobby Lynn said quickly.

Was that all? I laughed.

"Do you know?" Rosemary said.

"Only One Question!" I reminded her. "Sure I know. He was a soldier and he loved my mother very much. He planned to marry her—I know he did—but he was killed at Pearl Harbor five months before I was born."

Sure it was a lie. Somehow I couldn't tell them he went away right after Pearl Harbor was bombed and never even wrote a letter, like my mama and I did not matter at all.

"That's all," I said. "Except for his name—Ernest Bevins."

"That's so sad," Rosemary said.

Then she mumbled it was her turn. Our One Question for Rosemary was something Bobby Lynn and I had wondered about a lot.

"Have you and Roy done it?"

Rosemary grinned.

"Yeah" was all she said, and too late we realized our mistake. She didn't have to tell us anything else because we asked a yes/no question. Bobby Lynn and I looked at each other, disgusted, and Rosemary laughed and laughed.

"Okay." She yielded at last. "I'll say more. We did it three times during football season. I wanted to beat Clintwood so bad, I promised Roy if he would make a touchdown, I'd do it."

"And he did!" Bobby Lynn said.

"And he made two more touchdowns after that," Rosemary said with a smile. "One against Bristol and one against Richlands."

We giggled.

"But after football season I wouldn't do it anymore."

"Why not?"

"I was afraid of getting in trouble."

"Well, I have heard," I said, "that once you start doing it, you can't stop."

"That is a great big lie," Rosemary said. "It was easy to stop. And I am through till I'm married. It's not all it's cracked up to be, you know."

It was midnight before we got to bed. Bobby Lynn and Rosemary shared Grandpa's big bed that night, and I slept in the bed where I was born, and where I slept with Mama until I was three years old. I opened up the window all the way to let in the gentle night breeze. The homemade quilt, stitched by the hands of my Grandmother Lambert, was fully visible in the moonlight. It was a sunburst pattern in bright yellow and red. Lovingly I ran my hand over it and wondered about the woman who put it together. Was she in love with my Grandpa Lambert?

Nessie settled down with a sigh on the rug and I stretched out on the bed. I looked down at my body, firm and pretty in the moonlight. Yes, I thought, I have arrived. I have reached womanhood, and I am not ashamed of these feelings I have for Jesse. We want each other and it is as simple and natural as that. Then why this feeling of anxiety? Why do I hesitate to do what he wants me to do? I fell into an uneasy sleep.

It was not the bright moonlight that woke me, nor

the shadow of the weeping willow sweeping my pillow. It wasn't even the rich, heavy scent of honeysuckle that hung like something solid in the air. But I was aware of all these things as I rolled over and opened my eyes to the night. It was something else—something more subtle, illusive.

"What is it?" I whispered.

Then I saw her shadow interwoven among the shadows of the weeping willow. Sweeping . . . swaying . . . moving rhythmically with the pendent branches ever so gently across the wall, the bed, and my face on the pillow.

*Willa, Willa, on my pilla' . . .*

Quietly I moved to the window and looked out. It was Willa in a long, full, lacy white gown dancing around the willow tree in the moonlight.

"Willa!" I whispered, laughing, and she looked at me and winked.

She went on dancing, breathlessly beautiful, and graceful as a swan with her lovely red hair floating about her.

"Willa," I said again softly, and she came to the window, laughing mischievously, and knelt. We sat there, one on either side of the window, our arms touching on the windowsill, looking into each other's eyes. I could smell her honeysuckle breath as she panted slightly. Her cheeks were full and red.

"You feel it, too, don't you, Willa?"

She rolled her eyes toward the moon, and smiled mysteriously.

"Is it the spring?" I said. "Or is it the moon? Is it that old black magic, Willa?"

She looked steadily into my eyes.

"Or is it just a trick?" I whispered to her, and the breeze caught my words and lifted them into the night. "Is falling in love just a trick that nature plays on us?"

She said nothing.

"I want to be sure, Willa. I'm going to wait until I'm sure it's the right thing to do."

The next day I said no to Jesse.

# TWENTY-TWO

⋈ Just as I figured, the weeks following were so frantic not a one of us had time to spit. At the crack of dawn we rolled out of bed. And up on the mountain with the sky right on top of you, dawn seemed to crack earlier than it did down in the bottom.

We were grumpy as we ate bread and jelly or something left over from the night before. We each took a pan full of water—cold because none of us wanted to build a fire to heat it. I went off to my bedroom, Rosemary to the other, and Bobby Lynn took the kitchen, and we washed ourselves as best we could, shivering, shaking, and scratching bug bites. You'd be surprised how fast you can wash yourself under those conditions.

Then we dressed, piled into the pickup, and rode

the twelve miles to school, where we dragged through the day, feeling grungy.

Right after school we changed into our shorts and tennis shoes and headed for the patch. Along with Aunt Evie, Mama, Luther, Beau, and Phyllis, Cecil and his brothers and sisters, and sometimes Roy, we all picked until our fingers were crimson and our backs in pain. Then Mama and Cecil took the berries down the mountain. That week Mama struck a deal with the A & P and the coal company store in Ruby Valley. Both stores wanted all we could pick. We had hit the big time. Mama handled all the money and kept track of how many quarts everybody picked. She made a rule also that "a nickel on every quart goes to Tiny 'cause this is Tiny's land and Tiny's strawberries. Without her, none of us would be making any money."

Her saying that made me feel important, but self-conscious, too. I never had told my friends about my land because we never bragged to each other.

"You own all this?" Bobby Lynn said, sweeping her arms around the mountaintop.

"Yeah, my Grandpa Lambert left it to me."

"*You*? Just *you*?" Rosemary said. "Not your whole family?"

"No, just me."

"Wow!"

They looked at each other and grinned. "That's cool, Tiny."

Cool. I would have to remember that word. Everybody was saying it. Yeah, it was cool, thanks to Grandpa Lambert.

At the end of three weeks we were plum picked out,

and we didn't leave many strawberries on the ground that year. We counted up our money and squealed. Rosemary and Bobby Lynn made just over $100.00 each and I made $160.00. It was the most I had ever made on strawberries.

Saturday afternoon, Rosemary drove us down to the Clevingers' to get the Henry J.

Mrs. Clevinger was hanging out clothes in her back yard.

"My goodness, just look at you little brown boogers and it ain't even June yet!"

We crowded around the Henry J. It was olive-green, six years old, and not a scratch in sight. Only problem was Bobby Lynn and I couldn't drive, but Rosemary was going to teach us.

Then a funny thing happened. Bobby Lynn's daddy drove up. He looked handsome, wearing a dark suit, a white shirt, and a tie. Bobby Lynn got the strangest look on her face when she saw him, like she wanted to laugh and cry at the same time. She walked out to him and they fell into each other's arms, and started to cry, both of them. I never loved Bobby Lynn more than at that moment. I knew somehow exactly how she felt, seeing her daddy like that for the first time in months. I had to turn away and look at something else because I wanted to cry, too. How wonderful it must be, I thought, to have a daddy like that—a real daddy. And the way he cried when he hugged her—gosh, I loved him for that.

Mrs. Clevinger was standing watching them and she had tears in her eyes, too.

Rosemary cleared her throat and poked me.

"Let's get out of here."

"Okay."

So Rosemary went over and said to Mrs. Clevinger, "If you'll give me the key, me and Tiny will go for a ride and leave y'all alone for a while."

"Oh, I'll go, too," she said quickly. "He came to see Bobby Lynn."

She gave the key to Rosemary.

"Be back directly," she called to Bobby Lynn and her daddy.

They were coming across the yard with their arms around each other.

"There's iced tea in the Frigidaire," she continued, and waved.

Mr. Clevinger looked at us, and smiled, but Bobby Lynn didn't seem to see or hear a thing, except her daddy.

"Come in the house, Daddy," she said.

Mrs. Clevinger climbed in the back seat and looked away toward the courthouse steeple. Rosemary got in the driver's seat with me beside her. We headed out of town and down the river toward Kentucky. I was excited to be in the Henry J. I kept looking for somebody we knew from school so we could stop and show off our car.

"I know everybody's blaming me," Mrs. Clevinger said suddenly after we had been driving for about five minutes.

Rosemary and I exchanged glances.

"For what, Miz Clevinger?" I said.

"For breaking up the family," she said. "They're all talking about me."

"I don't think so," Rosemary said.

"Oh yeah, they are. But I didn't want to be married anymore. I couldn't stand it no more."

"Why not?" I said and turned around to look at her.

She appeared very childish sitting there gazing out the window with one hand hanging out. She watched the passing hills.

"Well, if you could stay in love, it wouldn't be so bad," she said. "But you don't stay in love, you know. Nobody does."

That puzzled me, but I didn't say anything out loud. I was thinking, Of course people stay in love. I knew Jesse and I would always be in love. And what about Roy and Rosemary?

But to my surprise Rosemary said, "I know what you mean, Miz Clevinger."

"Do you, Rosemary? Slim and me, we were your age, you know—kids. And we were so love-sick we didn't know beans!"

Ahead of us there was a crowd of people gathered by the river at the mouth of Bull Creek. Rosemary slowed down so we could see what was going on. It was the Holy Rollers gathered for a baptism.

"Oh, let's stop and watch," I said.

I liked to see them carrying on when they came out of the water. Rosemary pulled off the road and parked.

"Everybody says a woman can't be happy without a man," Mrs. Clevinger went on. "But I'll swaney, I'm happier now than I ever was married to Slim."

The Holy Rollers were singing:

*Yes, we'll gather at the river,*
*The beautiful, the beautiful river,*
*Gather with the saints at the river*
*That flows by the throne of God.*

About a dozen people were draped in white robes and lined up to be ducked by the preacher.

"I wish I didn't feel so guilty about Bobby Lynn. She's embarrassed, and she misses her daddy," Mrs. Clevinger said.

"Let's walk down to the water," Rosemary said.

So we got out of the car and walked down through the weeds, which were coated with coal dust, and our legs got dirty. Mrs. Clevinger lifted her frock above her knees.

We watched the preacher and his helper baptize the people one by one "in the name of the Father, the Son, and the Holy Ghost." Then they came out of the water shouting.

"He worshed away my sins," an old woman said as she hugged us all.

"Git shed of thy guilt, sinner!" the preacher was crying. "Git shed of it all today!"

"I will!" Mrs. Clevinger said loudly. Startled, we turned to look at her. "I want to be baptized."

"Haven't you been baptized?" Rosemary whispered to her, obviously embarrassed.

"Not like this. I want to be baptized in the river!" she announced.

"Come on, sister, come with me," a woman said, placing her arm around Mrs. Clevinger, and leading her away.

"Oh boy . . ." Rosemary mumbled.

"Won't you join your mother, young'uns?" an old man said to us.

"Our mother? Oh . . . no. No thanks," I said.

Everybody was looking at us, and we were self-conscious. We watched the huddle of women where Mrs. Clevinger had disappeared. Very soon she reappeared wearing one of the white robes. She had her arms folded neatly across her chest in the form of an X. The women led her to the river, and when she waded out in the water to join the preacher, the robe ballooned out around her and floated on top of the water. The sun was shining on the water, throwing rainbows and halos all around the people in the water, including Mrs. Clevinger with her blond hair a-flutter and her robe floating around her. Why, she looked like an angelic little girl.

"I don't believe my dad-burned eyes," Rosemary said.

"Me neither." I stifled a giggle as the whole thing suddenly struck me as funny. I choked.

"Shut up!" Rosemary punched me.

"I baptize you, Violet Clevinger, in the name of the Father . . ."

And he ducked her.

The people started singing and clapping their hands.

*Oh, Beulah Land! Sweet Beulah Land!*
*As on the highest mount I stand,*
*I look away across the sea*
*Where mansions are prepared for me*

*And view the shining glory shore,*
*My heaven, my home forevermore.*

Some shouted, others spoke in tongues, and still others lay down and rolled around on the riverbank in religious ecstasy. It was this ceremony that earned them the name of Holy Rollers.

Mrs. Clevinger came up gasping. The cold water had knocked the breath out of her. I remembered that some of the holler families channeled their sewage into the river, but I quickly pushed that thought away.

Her hair looked dark now and clung tightly to her head and neck. The women hurried her back into the huddle, and shortly she emerged again in her own clothes.

She came back to us then, waving and smiling at the crowd. They were clapping for her like she was a celebrity, and she was acting like one!

"I'm ready to go now," she said to us.

So we went to the Henry J. Rosemary turned us around and we headed for Black Gap.

"I'm just not cut out to be a wife," Mrs. Clevinger went on as if our conversation had not been interrupted at all. "Not everybody is."

That did it.

I had the giggles.

Rosemary slapped me on the thigh.

"Shut up!"

But it was too late.

"We only got married because we thought we had to," Mrs. Clevinger confessed, unaware that I was in the throes of a fit. "And then it turned out to be a false alarm."

Rosemary smiled then, and I thought, Oh no, here it comes. She's going to get tickled, too.

"I don't know how it happened," Mrs. Clevinger went on. "I just woke up one morning and realized I was an old married woman and I didn't like it. I remember thinking, How did I get here? What hit me?

"I felt like I had been . . . well . . . hypnotized or something. And I was just coming out of it. That night I looked at Slim and I thought, 'Who is he? That's not the cute boy I married. This man's feet stink, and he belches, and sometimes he pees in the back yard!' "

That's when Rosemary and I both sputtered all over the dashboard, and Mrs. Clevinger caught it, too.

Thus we entered a season of laughter—the summer of 1959.

# TWENTY-THREE

≽ Jesse graduated from high school and went to work for his daddy in Big Lick. Cecil and Roy got summer jobs helping to build a church. But on weekends the six of us still got together. Lots of times we went to the drive-in show down at the mouth of Glory. We took our blankets and spread them out on the ground under the stars where we ate popcorn and drank pop while watching Rock Hudson in *Magnificent Obsession* or Debbie Reynolds as Tammy or Charlton Heston as Moses, or Doris Day as Julie. We liked scary pictures, too, like *Donovan's Brain*. That was a good one. We watched Lana Turner and Sandra Dee in *Imitation of Life* about seven times, and Rosemary, Bobby Lynn, and I cried every single time. The boys would act like they were puking.

Then all of a sudden Bobby Lynn started dating Richard Sutherland and Cecil started dating Judy Thornbury, but they stayed good friends and our crowd grew to eight. I thought that was really odd because I knew doggone good and well if Jesse and I broke up (which would never happen, of course), one of us would have to leave the crowd, and it would not be me. I said so, but Jesse didn't say anything.

Sometimes on Saturday or Sunday afternoon we all drove over to the Breaks of the Cumberland or to Hungry Mother park and cooked hot dogs or hamburgers outside. We also skated a lot at the new roller rink in Black Gap, and cruised the CAR-feteria.

Rosemary taught me and Bobby Lynn how to drive. And did we drive! We got our licenses. We followed dirt roads and gravel roads and paved roads up every little creek and holler and ridge and branch in southwest Virginia. It was a golden summer, and we were three seventeen-year-old girls with a car. We each took turns keeping it for a week at a time. We were just full of ourselves. We went lots to the new county pool, where we learned to swim and dive and bake our bodies like city girls.

We hiked up Ruby Mountain and picnicked by the spring. On the few rainy days we hung around the Sweet Shop in Black Gap, eating enormous gobs of repulsive stuff.

But most of all, we laughed. We laughed the summer away, and did nothing naughtier than discuss the three times Roy and Rosemary did it.

When September rolled around, we began our senior year. We got more heys in the mornings than anybody else in school. Rosemary, Bobby Lynn, and I even set some of the trends, like plucking our eyebrows and wearing dimes in our penny loafers. I figure we were absolutely the cockiest bunch of seniors ever to go through Black Gap High School.

About that time, Jesse stopped coming around so much. He said his job kept him busy and tired. But I started wondering about him when he didn't come to any of our football games. I didn't think anything could stop him from coming to watch Roy, Cecil, and Richard, who were big stars that year, play football. Somebody told me they saw him at a Big Lick game one Friday night, but he told me he had stayed home that night. Well, I thought, it's not important.

One weekend he said he wanted to "borrow" his class ring back from me to have it cleaned. The following weekend he said he couldn't see me Friday or Saturday night, and I really began to wonder. On Saturday night I called Bobby Lynn.

"Do you think Jesse's mad at me about something, Bobby Lynn?" I said.

"I don't know. Why don't you dump him, Tiny?"

"Dump him? What brought that on?"

"Cecil says Jesse doesn't deserve you, Tiny. I feel the same way."

"Cecil? What's going on, Bobby Lynn? I feel like everybody knows something I don't know."

"Did you know Cecil and Judy broke up last night?" She changed the subject quickly.

"No, how come?" I said.

188 / RUTH WHITE

"I don't know the details, but I bet it was on account of you."

"Me? What're you talking about?"

"Judy's always been jealous of you because Cecil talks about you all the time."

"Oh, he does not! Me and Cecil are like brother and sister. Judy knows that. I'm in love with Jesse."

"I know, I know," she said, sighing.

"What does that mean?"

"Nothing. Listen, Tiny, I gotta go. Richard's coming over."

"No! Something's going on. Tell me!"

Bobby Lynn was quiet, and I found my heart was pounding wildly. Somewhere deep inside, I knew what was coming.

"Tell me, Bobby Lynn."

"You sure you want to hear what I got to say about Jesse Compton?"

There were ice particles in my blood veins, tinkling against each other, and I found myself shivering.

"Tell me," I croaked.

"Well, Tiny, Jesse has a girl in Honaker. He's been seeing her off and on for a month. Now I think it's more on than off."

No, no, no, no . . .

Jesse loved me. Why would Bobby Lynn tell me such lies? Jesse would never hurt me like that.

"Tiny, you okay?"

"Yeah. Bobby Lynn, who told you that?"

"Everybody knows it, Tiny. I wanted to tell you before, but nobody would let me."

Everybody knows it. Everybody. Everybody but

Tiny. Blind, stupid Tiny. Tiny who believed that people stay in love forever. But no, it's a lie. No, no, no . . .

"Say something, Tiny."

"I don't believe you, Bobby Lynn. Why are you doing this?"

"Tiny, come down to earth! It's true!"

"No, it's a lie."

And I hung up. I sleep-walked upstairs and lay down on my bed, numb and oh, so cold. I wrapped myself up in a quilt and looked out at the gray sky.

Jesse had said he was helping his daddy tonight. Why not call him?

It was starting to rain, just a drizzle. And the hills were barely tinged with red and gold. Soon winter would be coming and my world would be gray and bleak . . .

No, Jesse, no . . .

I lay there, in shock, in denial as the evening light failed me and darkness clutched me in its black, cold fingers.

It would be so easy to call him. Then I would know for sure.

It wasn't supposed to happen this way. If he knew how hurt I was, he would come to me, beg my forgiveness, hold me . . .

Yes, I would call. And I would tell him what Bobby Lynn said. Of course he would tell me it was all a pack of lies, and I would never speak to Bobby Lynn again.

It was 8:30 p.m. I went downstairs and dialed his number with shaking fingers.

"Mrs. Compton, is Jesse there?"

"Oh, hi, Tiny. No, Jesse's gone out."

"Oh . . . oh, where to, Mrs. Compton? Do you know where he's gone to?"

She hesitated.

"I'm not sure, Tiny, but I think I heard him say he was going to Honaker."

"Honaker?"

I was stunned, devastated, terrified.

"Yeah, that's where he went—Honaker."

"Oh" was all I could say. Just "Oh."

"Can I give him a message, Tiny?"

"Yeah. Tell him to call me when he comes in."

"Tonight, you mean? It'll be late, Tiny."

"That's okay. Tell him to call me no matter what time it is."

"Well, okay."

I stood by the telephone, frozen.

On the television I could hear the *Perry Como Show* song requesting letters from viewers.

Yes, that's what I would do. I would write Jesse a letter just like I used to write to Mr. Gillespie.

*Dear Jesse:*

*Maybe it's true and maybe it's a lie what they are saying about you. If it's true, I don't want to know. I don't care. If you will come back to me I will do anything you want me to do. I will not ever mention the girl in Honaker. I will forgive you. I just want things to be like they used to be. I love you so much.*

*Love, Tiny*

*XOXOXOXOXOXOXOXOXOXOXO*

I kissed the letter and sealed it and put it under my pillow. Then I lay awake in a kind of stupor for hours, waiting for him to call. But he didn't call. Not that night. Not the next day, which was Sunday, nor Sunday night. And the truth began to eat away around the edges of my blind hope. Late Sunday night I tore up the letter and flushed it. No, I would not beg. Not that I was above it. No, I was afraid Jesse would be ashamed of me. Somehow, somehow I had to keep my head up even when it hurt so bad I couldn't stand it.

At school on Monday I managed to act almost normal. Bobby Lynn had the good sense not to mention our conversation. Twice I caught Cecil watching me, studying my face, and when I looked into his eyes he turned away. Everybody knew. And now I knew, too.

That night I called Jesse.

"Oh, hi, Tiny," he said. "What's up?"

"Hi, Jesse. Did you get my message?"

"Oh . . . yeah. I got it."

"Well, you didn't call. Anything wrong?"

My hands were sweating on the phone.

"No, I've been busy, that's all."

"Bobby Lynn told me something about you, Jesse. I just wonder if it's true."

"What'd she say?"

"She said you have a girl in Honaker."

Jesse didn't say a word.

"Is it true, Jesse?"

"Yeah, Tiny. I didn't know how to tell you."

The silence between us was awful to hear, and it went on and on.

"Well," I said at last, "what now?"

"I don't know. I'll call you, Tiny, okay?"
I couldn't speak.
"Okay, Tiny? I'll call you?"
"Okay, Jesse. Call me."
"Take it easy, Tiny."
"Yeah."
And my world came to an end.

# TWENTY-FOUR

⅄ Jesse didn't call again. It took only a week for Vern to figure out what had happened.

"Where's lover boy?" he asked at supper the next Saturday night.

I didn't answer.

"Flew the coop, huh?" He laughed.

This is what he had been hoping for.

"Did y'all bust up?" Mama said.

I didn't answer her either. The pain was raw, like an open wound, and maybe they saw it in my face because they didn't say anything else.

Of course, it was Aunt Evie who I spilled my guts to. If it hadn't been for her I think I would have died. With her I cried out loud and poured all my misery upon her shoulders. Because I knew if anybody would understand, she would. And I was not disappointed. She comforted me like no one else could. Every tear I shed was wiped away by a loving word or touch. But nothing could make the pain go away, and I thought I would feel like this forever. Look at Aunt Evie. It was fifty years ago that Ward jilted her, and still she suffered.

I couldn't sleep. For hours I lay awake beside Phyllis and watched the light change outside from gray to black to dull purple as morning came, and the earth changed from gold to drab gray as winter came back to grieve me more.

I went over and over in my mind all the things Jesse and I said to each other last summer, all the things we did together, the fun we had, the way we laughed and held hands and kissed. And I imagined his coming back to me, what he would say, how we would kiss and make up.

Sometimes I saw Willa sitting quietly silhouetted in the window looking out at the sad hills. A shadowy, wispy figure she was in the dark with her hair plaited in one long thick braid down her back. She didn't say anything because she felt sad, too. She was just hanging around in case I needed her.

The rains came down all through December. The hills dripped into the soggy bottom, and the mud thickened and deepened, black with coal.

On New Year's Eve I was sitting listening to the radio when the phone rang and it was Jesse. I was so stunned I couldn't speak. How many times I had dreamed of this moment!

"How've you been, Tiny?" he said.

"Fine," I said.

That's all I could think of to say.

"Well, I just called to say goodbye."

"Where you goin' to?"

"To the air force. I'm leaving for Harlingen, Texas, first thing tomorrow morning."

"The air force? When did this come about, Jesse?"

"Since I broke up with Barbara. I decided I don't want to hang around here anymore, and I don't want to be a welder. So I'm getting out."

I was silent.

"And I wanted to say I'm sorry for the way things turned out between you and me," he went on.

"Forget it."

"No, I was kinda rough on you. You would never have treated me like that."

That was the truth.

"So maybe we can be friends, huh, Tiny?"

"Sure, Jesse. Write to me."

"I'll do it. You take care of yourself, and maybe I'll see you in the spring."

"Yeah, 'bye, Jesse."

The next night, when I knew he was gone to Texas, I was wide awake again most of the night remembering, regretting, hurting. Every time I closed my eyes I could see us dancing around the fire on the mountaintop. And the old Red Wing song kept going around in my head.

*She loved a warrior bold, this shy little maid of old,*
*But brave and gay, he rode one day to battle far away.*

Just like my real daddy, I was thinking. Running off to play war games and leaving broken hearts at home.


*Now, the moon shines tonight on pretty Red Wing,*
*The breeze is sighing, the night bird's crying,*
*For afar 'neath his star her brave is sleeping,*
*While Red Wing's weeping her heart away.*


"Jesse . . . Jesse . . . come back!"

Early on a Saturday morning I drifted in and out of sleep. Outside, somebody was yodeling, and I remembered those Saturday mornings when I was in the ninth grade and Bobby Lynn took yodeling lessons from Aunt Evie, and I could hear them up there. The yodeling was pretty. I fantasized that it was Jesse yodeling for me, and I saw myself go to the window and raise it, and yodel in return.

I opened my eyes. A cold, white sun was trying to come into my bedroom, and I got up and looked out. There was a light snow. The yodeling had ended and its echo bounced off the hills. No one was in sight. Did I dream it?

The house was cold and damp. I put on britches, a sweater, and a pair of socks and shoes. Then I went downstairs.

Phyllis was sitting at the kitchen table eating a fried apple pie. Nessie lay at her feet, but she came to me wagging her tail when she saw me.

"Hello, my lamb chops," I crooned and petted her.

"Are you going somewhere today, Tiny?" Phyllis asked me.

"No."

"Will you play with me?"

I fixed a bowl of corn flakes and sat down beside her.

She was ten years old now, nearly eleven, almost as tall as me, and as developed as a thirteen-year-old. We hadn't talked much in a long time.

"Play with you? Ain't you too big for that stuff?"

"What stuff?"

"Playing is little-girl stuff."

"We could play cards."

"Where's Beau and Luther? They'll play with you."

"But I want you to play with me, Tiny."

At that moment her hands came into view, and I was horrified. All her nails were chewed down to the quick, and all around them the skin was torn away.

"What on earth have you gone and done to your fingernails?" I hollered at her.

She tried to hide her hands, but I grabbed one hand and forced it open.

"Lordy, Phyllis. I never saw the beat!"

She jerked away from me.

"Leave me alone!" she said.

"Has Mama seen your nails?"

"I dunno." She shrugged and stuck out her lower lip.

"Where's Mama now?" I said. "I think she orta see what you've gone and done to yourself."

"She went to the hospital again. She's always gone with Dixie."

It was the truth. Mama just loved to hang around the hospital with the sick people. She wanted to get a job there as a nurse's aide, but I heard Vern yelling at her about her wanting to work for slave wages. He said people would think he couldn't support his family. I saw Mama grit her teeth when he said that.

"Well, we'll doctor up your nails, then I'll play you a game of rummy or something. First, though, I'm going up to see Aunt Evie."

"She's got company," Phyllis said.

"Who in the world?"

"I dunno. Some old man. He come up the road yodeling."

I dropped my spoon. No, it couldn't be.

"Yodeling? Did Aunt Evie yodel back?"

"She shore did. She come out on the porch and yodeled at him."

"Phyllis!"

"What'sa matter?"

"Don't you see? It musta been Ward!"

"Naw, Tiny. That's just a story she tells. Ward's never really coming back . . . is he?"

"Well, who else would be yodeling to her?"

We looked at each other.

"Is he still up there?"

"I reckon. I never did see him leave. Wouldn't that be something, Tiny? I mean, if he should come back after all these . . . how many years?"

"About fifty years come spring."

"And what if they get married?"

I smiled as I pictured Aunt Evie in a white wedding dress.

"I guess stranger things have happened, Phyllis," I said. "But I don't know what."

For the next half hour we watched Aunt Evie's shack out the kitchen window. Finally, here he came: an old man with a white beard and a cane. He paused on the porch, slung a pack up over his back, and turned around and said something to Aunt Evie, who was standing in the doorway. She put up her hand like she was saying goodbye. Then he left. We watched him walk down the path around our house and to the road below.

I hurried out the door and up the hill with Phyllis right behind me. Aunt Evie was still standing on the porch watching the old man. And her face looked the most peculiar I ever had seen it look. There was a whole new something-or-other in her eyes.

"Who was that man?" Phyllis and I said together.

"Hit was Ward, my man, in the flesh," she said, then turned and went back inside.

Phyllis and I exchanged a glance and followed Aunt Evie inside.

"Well, tell us about it, Aunt Evie. Tell us everything!"

We were so excited we were hopping up and down. But Aunt Evie was as calm as a spring night. She started piddling around in a drawer looking for something.

"There ain't a thang to tell," she said as simply as that. "He come in and set down and said, 'Howdy, Evelyn' . . . He always did call me Evelyn, and hit's not even my name. My name's Evie . . . just Evie. 'How are ya?' he said.

"And I said, 'Where the hell you been?'

" 'Here and there,' he said. 'But now I'm here to stay.' "

Aunt Evie fell silent as she kept looking for something in the drawer.

"Did you lose something, Aunt Evie?" I said.

"My specs," she said. "They was right 'cheer."

"There they are," Phyllis said. "Right beside your hand."

"Oh," Aunt Evie said as she picked up the glasses and put them on. "If hit had been a snake, hit woulda bit me," she said, and closed the drawer.

Then she started reading a piece of paper she had crumpled up in her hand. Phyllis and I smiled at each other.

"What's that you're reading?" I said.

"A pome he said he writ fer me. But he never writ hit a'tall. I read hit somewheres else before. He always was the biggest liar!"

And she tossed the paper in the stove. Phyllis and I exchanged glances again. Never had we heard any criticism of the legendary Ward before today.

"Then what happened?" Phyllis said. "You said to him, 'Where the hell you been?' and then . . ."

I gouged Phyllis. "Don't say that word."

Aunt Evie sat down at the table, took off her glasses,

and carefully laid them down. I sat on one side of her and Phyllis on the other.

"Well, I looked at him, and I thought, Lordy, I don't know this man a'tall. I never did know him. He's a stranger I been pining after for fifty years. And I don't want him no more'n I want the measles."

"It's because he's old, Aunt Evie," I said. "He's still your Ward."

"No, he ain't. He never was my Ward. My Ward was somebody I made up outa my head. He never existed."

"What d'you mean?"

"Lord, child, I mean I've been a fool. I could have married Clint Clevinger and been Bobby Lynn's grandma. But no, I said if I couldn't have Ward, I wouldn't have nobody. I thought Ward was my one and only. Now I know, Tiny, after all these wasted years. There's no such thing as a one and only! No such thing!"

"You mean you think you coulda loved somebody else if you had tried to?" I asked.

"That's the gist of hit! And he shore weren't worth pining over—not for a month, much less fifty years!"

She sighed heavily.

Could it be true? Could it be possible to fall in love more than once? Could it be that someday I would think of Jesse as a stranger? And that I would be able to let go just like that? Was it possible?

We stayed with Aunt Evie for about an hour and let her talk about her own self for a change. She was a pitiful old thing, and didn't know what to do with

the rest of her life. She didn't know how to do anything
but wait for Ward. Then she said she had to go help
Mrs. Rife do some sewing. So Phyllis and I went home.

Vern was sitting in the kitchen drinking bourbon.

"Where's Beau and Luther?" Phyllis said.

"I took 'em up to Dad's. Where you girls been?"

"Up to Aunt Evie's."

"Rosemary called you, Tiny," he said. "Wants you
to call her."

I went to the hall and dialed Rosemary's number.
Phyllis and Nessie went upstairs.

"Hi, gal," Rosemary said. "Want to go sledding?"

"Sledding? There's not enough snow for sledding."

"Over at the Breaks there is. There's lots of snow
there."

"Okay. Who all's going?"

"Me and you and Cecil and Bobby Lynn and
Richard."

"What about Roy?"

"I didn't ask him."

"Why not?"

"I don't have to take him with me everywhere I go."

"Oh. Well, I'll ride over with Cecil."

I hurried upstairs. Phyllis was sitting by the window
in Willa's spot, looking at the hills.

"Where ya goin' to, Tiny?" she said.

"To the Breaks, sledding."

"Can I go?"

"No. You know you're too young to hang around
with my crowd, Phyllis."

"Please, Tiny."

I looked at her as I wiggled into my boots. She was

chewing her nails and looking at me with pleading eyes.

"No, Phyllis, you know you can't go. What's the matter with you?"

She didn't answer. I put on my scarf and gloves, then slipped on my heavy jacket. I would have to dig the sled out of Beau and Luther's closet. I looked at Phyllis again. She sure was acting funny.

"Get your hands out of your mouth," I said to her.

"I won't get out of the car." She made another desperate attempt. "And I won't say a word."

This was not like Phyllis a'tall, and as I stood puzzling over it, I saw two big tears bubble up in her eyes.

"Don't leave me here with Daddy!" she sobbed suddenly.

Oh God, my sister, my sister!

I went to her and took her into my arms. I held her close to my heart and rocked her and crooned to her while she cried and cried. I cried, too, as I remembered those awful days, and how I had yearned for comfort.

Oh, my sister, my sister. Why didn't I see this coming? I was so wrapped up in my own problems.

"He said he would kill Nessie if I told," Phyllis choked. "Do you think he will?"

"No! He will not hurt Nessie! I won't let him. And he won't ever hurt you again, Phyllis, I promise."

She slumped in my arms. I would hold her as long as she wanted me to, all day if necessary. And all the while my mind was racing. I would tell. Nothing would stop me now. Nothing. It didn't matter who knew. He would never hurt me or Phyllis again. I would tell Mama, and if she wouldn't do anything,

then I would tell Mr. Gillespie. He would do something. I knew there was a law against what Vern did.
He was scared of the law.

I took off my heavy clothes.

"I have to call Cecil," I told Phyllis. "But I'll be right
back."

"Promise?" she said.

"I promise. I am not going anywhere today."

"Sorry, Cecil," I said when I had him on the phone.
"Y'all go on and have a good time. Something important has come up."

"What's wrong, Tiny?"

"Nothing's wrong. I have to stay here, that's all," I
said.

"I can tell by your voice," he went on.

He knew me so well.

"Don't worry, Cecil. 'Bye now."

Then I went back upstairs to our room and closed
the door. We would stay there until Mama came home.
As I talked to Phyllis, I found out to my relief that
Vern did not actually rape her, but sooner or later he
was bound to try it if somebody didn't stop him.

Shortly after noon I heard Mama come in.

"You stay here, Phyllis," I said. "And I'll be right
back."

"Where ya goin' to?" she said.

"I'll be right back. You look after Nessie."

Mama was in her bedroom standing in her slip and
going through her closet for something to put on.

"You here?" she said when I walked in. "The house
is so quiet. Where's the young'uns?"

"Phyllis is in our room and the boys are at Grandpa Mullins's."

Mama found a housedress and slipped it on. I sat down on her bed.

"Mama, I got something real important to tell you," I said. "It's about Vern."

# TWENTY-FIVE

❧ The next evening found me, Phyllis, and Mama sitting quiet and still at the kitchen table, waiting. Mama was drinking coffee. Her eyes were so red and swollen from crying she couldn't see good. Phyllis's face was real pale and she felt bad. Nessie lay at my feet, quieter than usual and looking sad. The boys were still at Grandpa Mullins's house.

We were waiting for the preacher to finish talking to Vern. They were in the living room. Mama had called him late yesterday because she didn't know what else to do. Reverend Kermit Altizer was from an old-timey church in Black Gap. He didn't know us from

Adam's house cat, but we didn't have a regular church, so Mama picked him out of the telephone book.

My heart was heavier than it ever had been. Never before had there been so much crying and cussing, screaming and blaming in our house. Vern looked like he went back to childhood and thought his mama was going to whup him, and Phyllis wouldn't lift her eyes from the floor. She wouldn't let Nessie out of her sight. But it was Mama who worried me most. She seemed more helpless than ever, and I was disappointed in her. All she could do was whimper and cry. I thought she was cracking up. It was a nightmare, and I felt I was the only one who was awake and seeing things for real.

The temperature had plunged way down to freezing, and the weather man was calling for sleet and snow. It was a gray blanket all over my world.

I will take Phyllis and Nessie and run away, I was thinking. If they don't do something about Vern. If he gets away with this, he'll try it again. We can't live with him anymore.

About that time, Vern and the preacher walked in.

"Well, Mrs. Mullins." Reverend Altizer stood there smiling a crooked little smile at us. He had his dark Sunday suit and white shirt on, but his hair was greasy and he had long nicotine-stained fingernails with dirt under them.

"Let us have a moment of prayer," he said sweetly.

We bowed our heads and Reverend Altizer told God we were having a family problem and would he bless us. Then he prayed that we would be forgiving to one another and Christian in thought, word, and deed. Amen.

We looked at him, waiting.

"This is a most unfortunate situation," he said, still smiling.

Vern shuffled around the table and sat down beside Mama without looking at anybody.

"It appears that you and Mr. Mullins have had some problems in your marriage bed," he said to Mama.

That smile of his was getting on my nerves. Mama just looked at him with a blank face.

"Sometimes when a married man and woman don't get along, the children suffer," he went on. "A man in the prime of his life has certain needs, as you must surely know, Mrs. Mullins. And if the wife does not meet those needs, he must turn elsewhere."

Rage suddenly blinded me. He was taking Vern's part! But before I could explode, Mama rose up so fast and furiously her chair went crashing against the wall.

"Needs!" she cried, and that one word was like a gun going off. "Needs, you say!"

Never had I heard that tone of voice from Mama.

"And what about the needs of my young girls?"

I'll declare Mama grew a foot taller as she faced that preacher where he stood.

"They have needs, too! And they don't need no filthy old man forcing his lust on them!"

She stood there glaring and panting at that sleazy preacher, and that silly smile melted off his face at last.

"I just meant, Mrs. Mullins . . ."

"Don't say no more!" Mama yelled at him. "Just get your holy ass out of my kitchen before I get mad!"

The rest of us were rendered speechless. This was a new person we were seeing. Without another word the preacher left, and we were left sitting there with Mama towering over the room like the Statue of Liberty.

"And you!" She turned to Vern, and he seemed to shrivel up. "You have thirty minutes to get your clothes together and get out of this house, or I'll have you locked up so fast it'll make your head spin!"

"This is my house," Vern said lamely, but he was moving as he said it.

"No, it's *my* house and my children's house," Mama said. "Give us any trouble and you'll find yourself in jail."

Vern stood there, looking small. I was almost tempted to feel sorry for him, but I resisted.

"I love my girls," he said sadly. "That's the only reason I done it. I love them so much I couldn't help myself."

"Love!" Mama sputtered. "You make me sick! You hurt my girls worse than anybody ever did and you have the nerve to call it love!"

Suddenly she clutched the handle of a skillet there on the stove like she was aiming to clobber him. Vern backed toward the door, and I laid my hand on Mama's arm.

"Mama . . ."

She looked at me, let go of the skillet, and put her arm around me.

"I'm going to sue you for divorce," she said to Vern, "and get enough out of you to raise my young'uns by myself. Now git out of my sight!"

"What about my boys?" Vern whined. "I'm going to keep my boys."

"You bring 'em home to me! You ain't fit to raise 'em!"

Vern shuffled out of the room. Mama pulled Phyllis against her with her other arm and the three of us stood there together holding each other.

"How will I ever ever make it up to you?" she said with deep feeling.

"Oh, Mama," I said. "It wasn't your fault."

"Things are going to be different around here," she went on. "I promise. We're going to be a real family. I'm going to be a real mother."

"You're the best mother in the world," I said.

"My precious girls . . ."

Words failed her.

We sat down at the table.

"We have a lot to talk about," she said. "And I will never again let you down when you need me."

She was no longer crying, her head was up high, and there was a new air about her. I was very proud of her.

"I could have him locked up," she said. "But I don't think you would want everybody to know. You would be shamed before the world. You know how people talk, and you have suffered enough."

"That's true, Mama," I said. "It's the main reason I didn't tell anybody for so long."

We heard Vern leaving. Mama fixed a light supper for us, and we sat in the kitchen talking for hours. We started making plans for the future, and I felt this great flood of relief, exhilaration. My terrible secret was out, and Mama had defended me. I had protected my sister,

I didn't have to live in fear anymore, and Nessie slept peacefully at my feet.

The very next day, Mama got a job as a nurse's aide at the hospital. She would ride to work with Dixie.

The same day, Mama got legal separation papers. She asked for the house and twenty dollars a week child support. They would have to be separated for a year before she could file for divorce.

I was amazed at the turn of events. Our whole lives had changed in three days, and it had all clicked into place like it was meant to be.

The boys came home, but they were sullen. It's no telling what Vern said to them. Tuesday I found Luther alone in the kitchen reading a Superman comic. He was almost twelve, but small for his age. He was still a poor reader and a champion checkers player.

"Wanna play checkers, Luther?" I said to him. "Maybe I can beat you now."

"I don't want to do nothing with you," he said.

"What did I do?" I said and sat down with him, hoping we could talk.

"You told a pack of lies on my daddy."

"I did not lie, Luther."

"You're just a lying woman," he sneered. "Like my daddy said."

"Luther . . ."

But he left the room.

Beau was nearly thirteen and short and stumpy like Vern, but a whole lot smarter. He could read Shakespeare without stumbling, and he understood some of it.

But he wasn't speaking to me or Phyllis. He holed up in his room and came out only when he had to.

"They don't understand," Mama said. "Give 'em time. They'll come around."

Although Mama was real careful to save me and Phyllis from scorn—and I was proud of her for that—Phyllis was having a hard time handling everything that had happened. She felt like it was her fault that Mama ran Vern off. He was still her daddy, no matter what he did, and she still loved him. She stayed out of school that whole week with a sick headache. So I stayed with her. I read Nancy Drew to her, and fixed her good things to eat. I put an ice pack to her temples when she felt especially bad. When Mama came home in the evenings she sat with us and told us about her day at the hospital.

And we laid plans for the future. After graduation I would get a job at the bank or the insurance company because I had a year of typing. We would combine our strawberry money this year so that Mama could buy her own car, and I would teach her how to drive it.

By Saturday, Phyllis was better, and laughing at Snuffy Smith in the funny papers. And her cheeks were rosy again. Mama and I sat her down in the kitchen and trimmed her curly brown hair.

"You look exactly like Brenda Lee!" I told her because I knew how much she liked Brenda Lee.

"Oh, I don't!" she said, grinning.

"You do too! Don't she, Mama?"

"Exactly," Mama said. "Now, come on, Phyllis, let's

go upstairs and let me worsh your hair for you and roll it."

They left the kitchen and I fixed myself a bowl of rice pudding, and sat down at the table to eat it.

Cecil walked in.

"Hey, Tiny."

"Hey, Cecil. Want some pudding?"

"No thanks, Tiny. I got an important question to ask you."

"Okay, ask."

"Where's Vern?"

"That's not an important question."

"Well, where is he anyhow? He hasn't been home since Sunday and you haven't been in school and suddenly your mama has a job."

"You're nosy!" I said, laughing, but I knew he was concerned. Cecil thought about me a lot. "You might as well know Mama and Vern are getting a divorce, and that's all I have to say."

"A divorce?"

"Yeah, a divorce."

"Good!" he said matter-of-factly. "But that really wasn't my question. My important question is this: Will you go to the prom with me?"

"The prom? Cecil, it's January. The prom's not till April."

"I know. But I wanted to be sure nobody beat me to it."

"I don't expect you'll have a whole heap of competition. How come you to ask me? Why not Judy or Shelby or somebody like that?"

"You and I have been all through school together," he said. "And we've always been neighbors, and I have had this vision of you and me at the prom together."

I laughed.

"Cecil, you're funny."

He blushed then.

"Just for old times' sake, you know?" he said.

"Sure, Cecil. But remember, you're free to change your mind if you want to."

"Sure, and you too! I mean you can change your mind any time you want."

"Okay, it's a date."

Then he grinned real big, and didn't say anything. I had a feeling he was very pleased and relieved. Cecil had on his royal-blue football sweater, and it brought out the blue in his eyes, which were sparkling at the moment. He was definitely striking, I was thinking. Our eyes met then and suddenly I found myself wondering how it would feel to kiss Cecil. My face started burning, and I looked away.

For the first time in our lives, Cecil and I were uncomfortable together.

"Well, I'm glad that's settled," he said.

"Me too."

There was a great silence.

What was he thinking?

Cecil coughed.

"Did you know the Democrats are trying to run a Catholic for President?" he said lamely, desperately trying to pursue a conversation.

"Who is he?" I said.

"John Kennedy from Massachusetts."

"They'll never elect a Catholic for President," I said.

"They might."

"Naw, they won't."

The conversation died again. In the next moment, Cecil mumbled something and headed out the door, and I sat there puzzling over what had transpired.

# TWENTY-SIX

⇒ Mr. Gillespie still talked about the college down in the mountains of North Carolina. He wanted to interest somebody in applying there, but nobody paid him any mind. The town kids were all planning to attend some university or other, and the holler kids who were going anywhere at all were going to Radford Teachers' College or Bluefield Business College or somewhere like that. The rest of us were through with school.

But on a rainy Tuesday in February he asked me, Rosemary, and Bobby Lynn to stay after school, and he showed us this material he had on Mountain Retreat College.

"They have a superior music curriculum," Mr. Gillespie said. "And they are especially supportive of the average student who doesn't have much money."

I was looking out the window of the band room, watching the rain fall on the graveyard on the hill and remembering that first day I saw Mr. Gillespie. I couldn't bring up those feelings I had for him. Where did they go?

"My wife received a fine music education at Mountain Retreat," he said. "She's now teaching piano and voice lessons, and she loves it."

"It sounds like a dream come true," Rosemary said, as she poured over the M-R catalogue.

"I wish you three girls would think seriously about going there," he said.

"I want to," Rosemary said. "And Mama and Daddy want me to, too."

"What about Roy?" I said.

"What about him?" Rosemary said.

"He'll be hurt," Bobby Lynn said.

"Hurt because I want to better myself?" she said.

"What about you, Bobby Lynn?" Mr. Gillespie said.

"Mama and Daddy both want me to go to college, but I've never been too crazy about the idea."

"You have too much talent to waste!" Mr. Gillespie said. "You too, Tiny. All of you are gifted in different ways in music."

"Oh, it's too late to think about college now," Bobby Lynn said. "We'll never be accepted now."

"Sure you will. A small college like Mountain Retreat will accept students right up to the last minute. They always have vacancies. What about it, Tiny?"

"It's out of the question," I said. "I have to go to work the day after graduation."

They all looked at me. Everybody knew Vern was gone, I reckoned, but nobody ever asked me about him. As our meeting broke up, Rosemary was delirious with joy. She had made an important decision at last. And it looked like her marriage was on hold. She sent for an application to M-R that day.

At home I found a letter from Jesse waiting for me, but there wasn't much in it to excite me. He talked about his training and about Texas. It was signed "Sincerely, Jesse." But I answered it right then anyway. I tried to be warm and friendly and funny, and I signed it "Affectionately, Tiny." Then I began the endless wait for his next letter, which never came.

Rosemary received her application in a few days, filled it out, and sent it in. At lunch time, Bobby Lynn and I went through her M-R catalogue together. As I looked at the pictures I felt this vague kind of longing, something akin to homesickness, stirring in me. There it was—this perfect little school nestled snugly into a pocket of the mountains of North Carolina. All the buildings were made of rock, and they seemed to blend into the mountains like they grew there naturally. There were bright, pretty young people singing on an outdoor stage. There was a soccer field, a mountain trail leading straight up to the sky, a lake and waterfall that looked like they should be on a picture postcard, a covered bridge, a wishing well, a prayer room in the woods, and a big stone gate that said WELCOME TO MOUNTAIN RETREAT. Oh, how I envied Rosemary suddenly! I wanted to go there!

"I think I'll send in an application," Bobby Lynn said casually. "You know, just for the heck of it."

So she had the fever, too.

I plunged into depression. Never before had I been jealous of my two best friends. I was always happy for whatever good things came to them. But here they were ready to set out on the most glorious adventure of them all, into an enchanted world, and I was to be left behind. I took the catalogue home and tortured myself with it all evening. I tossed and turned for hours that night before I finally slept. Then I had a nightmare.

I woke up gasping, unable to recall what I was dreaming about. I wondered if I cried out in my sleep. The house was quiet and cold. The stoker must be out of coal.

There were tears on my cheeks, and I turned my face into the pillow. Would the nightmares go on forever? Would I ever get over it? Beside me, Phyllis sighed softly and turned over. I wondered if she had nightmares, too.

I reached out and found my heavy robe on a chair beside the bed. The M-R catalogue fell to the floor. I scooped it up, got out of bed, put on my robe and slippers, and went down to the kitchen, where I opened the oven door and turned it on to heat up the room. It was 2 a.m. I began to leaf through the catalogue again. Private voice lessons, it said, mixed chorus, orchestra . . .

Mama came into the kitchen.

"You okay, honey?" she said.

I looked up, surprised.

"Sure, why do you ask?"

"I heard you cry out, then I heard you get up. Nightmare?"

"Yeah, a little one."

She put her arm around me and I was touched.

"I think Beau and Luther forgot to fill up the stoker," I said. "The furnace is out."

"Yeah, well, I don't think we'll start it up again tonight. Want some cocoa?"

"Sure."

I watched her mix cocoa, sugar, and milk in a saucepan.

"What're you reading?" she said.

"Oh, just a catalogue from Mountain Retreat College."

"Is that the college where Rosemary is going?"

"Yeah, and Bobby Lynn, I think."

She looked at me.

"You want to go, too, don't you?" she said.

"I know it's out of the question," I said.

"Let me see that book," she said, and I handed it to her.

She read snatches of it, looked at the pictures, and made cocoa all at the same time. Finally she poured the cocoa into two cups and sat down with me at the table.

"This looks like a wonderful place," she said.

"It's almost nine hundred dollars a year," I said.

"That's not much when you consider room and board," she said.

"But I am going to work so I can help out here," I said.

"There must be a way," Mama said.

I felt a thrill of hope when she said that.

"You deserve to go if you want to," Mama said.

"Are you saying . . . ?"

"I'm saying we'll think of a way . . . somehow . . . something . . . I know you want to go."

"Oh, Mama." I about cried.

She patted my hand.

"Look at this little bridge . . . ain't it pretty?" she said.

"Look at the prayer room!" I said excitedly. "On page 31. It's even prettier!"

So together we went through the catalogue. She was almost as excited as I was at the possibility of my going to M-R.

"Somehow, Tiny," she said before we went back to bed, "we *will* manage. I promise. You *will* go!"

"Oh, Mama! Thank you!"

And I hugged her tight. Then I went back to bed and slept soundly.

The next day I couldn't wait to tell Rosemary and Bobby Lynn I was going to M-R with them. We hugged each other and squealed, and ran to tell Mr. Gillespie, who was pretty proud of himself. Then I sent for an application.

That night Mama took an old cigar box and wrote COLLEGE FUND on the top of it. Inside she dropped a ten-dollar bill and several ones from her purse. I added some ones from my own purse. Then we wrote ideas for raising money on little slips of paper and dropped them into the box. On one of them Mama wrote STRAWBERRY MONEY.

"But you have to have a car, Mama!" I said to her.

"No, I don't. I can go on riding with Dixie."

"But there's other places you have to go besides work."

"I'll manage. I'll get by."

Then my heart was heavy. I couldn't, in good conscience, take the strawberry money from Mama—maybe next year, but not this year. She really needed a car, and she would need it more with the Henry J gone. On another slip of paper I wrote SELL RUBY MOUNTAIN TO THE COAL COMPANY.

"No!" Mama said emphatically. "It would be like selling our souls."

The next day, Mr. Gillespie told me about the National Defense Education Act of 1958.

"You can borrow the money from the government —some of it anyway—and pay it back at a low rate of interest."

He helped me send for an application for that loan, and that night we put GOVERNMENT LOAN on a slip of paper and into the box.

"They also have work scholarships," Mr. Gillespie told me later. "That means you earn part of your keep by helping out there at the college. My wife worked there in the dining room."

That went into the box, too. My spirits rose higher and higher. The application arrived. I filled it out and sent it in, and waited. Rosemary, Bobby Lynn, and I dreamed a lot and talked incessantly about college.

"I think I'll ask Aunt Evie to come in and stay with us when you are gone," Mama said one night.

"That's a great idea!" I said. "She can cook and take care of the house and at the same time get out of that shack!"

"Yeah," Mama said. "We can be a lot of help to each other."

So it seemed to be working out for everybody.

"I'm going to miss you, Tiny," Phyllis said to me as she snuggled up to me on the couch, and put her cold, dirty feet on me just like always.

"I won't be gone forever," I said, placing an arm around her. "Promise me you will take good care of Nessie."

"Oh, I will!" she said. "Will you write letters to us?"

"You bet!"

We were all three accepted at M-R, but my spirits took another plunge. Even if I managed to scrape together nine hundred dollars, it seemed that was only the beginning. There were clothes and books, lab fees and recreation fees, travel expenses, car upkeep, extra fees for private lessons, spending money, and on and on.

"And what about next year?" I said to Mama. "And the year after that?"

"We'll worry about one year at a time!" Mama said. "Now, you stop that fretting!"

Then one day in March I got the surprise of my life. Mr. Norse, our principal, announced that the valedictorian for the class of 1960 was Cecil Hess! We were at an assembly and Cecil was sitting right beside me, and I about fainted. He turned and looked at me and smiled before he stood up to the applause.

Cecil! Valedictorian! Now, wasn't that just like him? I never knew his grades were that good. Never even suspected. Nobody did.

"So what are your plans?" I asked him that evening as we took a walk up the road. "Going to college?"

"Sure. I was accepted at the University of Virginia long ago. A full scholarship comes with the valedictorian honor."

"Cecil! Why didn't you tell me?"

"Oh, I don't know."

But I knew. I never asked him. I was never interested enough in Cecil to ask him much of anything, and he was never one to talk about himself. Look how I had taken him for granted! Sweet, dependable, agreeable Cecil, always there like a rock, a silent rock.

"What else don't I know about you, Cecil?" I said.

"There is one thing," he said and smiled mysteriously. "Maybe I'll tell you before we go away to college."

"What! Tell me now!"

He laughed.

"Okay, I'm really a prince in disguise. My father was the King of Somewhere-or-Other, and he wanted me to have a normal childhood, so . . ."

"So he sent you to live up a holler with a coal miner. Quite a sense of humor, that king!"

"Quite so!" he said, laughing.

"Really, tell me, Cecil."

"Someday, Tiny. Be patient."

I felt a strange flutter in the pit of my stomach.

The hills turned the brightest green and white and pink you can possibly imagine when spring arrived that year. I couldn't wait to get up in the mornings to look out the window. There was something new and fresh and magic coming into my heart along with the spring. The future looked brighter and more beautiful than ever it had before. For the first time in my life I could dream of myself doing something more than getting married and having babies. Maybe those things would be important someday, I told myself, but for now my own self mattered more to me than anything else, and it felt right. Then it occurred to me that sometimes I went whole days without thinking about Jesse. My wounds were healing.

All the windows were open and the fresh smells of spring were wafting through the house one morning in early April as I dressed for school.

"Local merchants have donated almost three hundred dollars in cash for the winner of the Fourth Annual Black Gap High School Talent Show," the radio announcer was saying. "It's the biggest jackpot ever for this event."

Three hundred dollars? Yes, three hundred dollars! That much money could go a long way toward solving my problems. And the talent show was still two weeks away. I trembled and sat down on the edge of my bed, and for the first time I allowed myself to remember completely last year's disgrace. It was so painful I had forced it out of my mind, vowing never again to subject myself to such humiliation.

But now, was God teasing me? I thought. Was he saying, "Get back up on that horse"? Did I dare try again? Suppose I failed again? Would I ever live it down?

# TWENTY-SEVEN

⊰ It was the biggest weekend of our senior year with the talent show on Friday night and the prom on Saturday night, and it was my week to drive the Henry J.

The prize money had grown to $375.00, and of course I had to go after that much money, so once again I entered the contest. The big night found me backstage with Bobby Lynn. I was wearing the blue dress from last year and my hair was done up in a French twist with little curls dangling around my face and neck. Everybody told me I looked pretty, which gave me confidence.

Cecil, Mama, Phyllis, Roy, and Rosemary were sitting out there on the front row. The boys hadn't

wanted to come. Behind them were a bunch of hillbillies from up Loggy Bottom whistling and hooting
at everybody who came onstage. One of their own, a
lanky ninth grader, was a contestant picking the banjo.
Maybe they figured if they made fun of everybody else,
their boy would look better.

And there were babies all over the place that night,
every single one of them crying or squealing. You never
heard such a noisy audience. And coughing! You
would think the lot of them had the whooping cough.
Besides all that, I knew they remembered me from last
year, and were all wondering if I would freeze up again.
Yes, I was pacing and nervous, but so far not petrified.
I simply could not stay out of the rest room. I had to
go again and again. That's where I was ten minutes
before my act, in a private stall, when I heard two other
girls talking as they entered the rest room.

"Did you hear about Tiny Lambert?"

"Yeah, about her stepfather raping her?"

"Yeah, everybody was talking about it in gym
today."

"He really raped her?"

"Yeah, can you imagine getting raped?"

"I bet it hurts."

"I bet she feels awful."

In a daze, I walked back to the wings where Bobby
Lynn was waiting.

Everybody knows. Everybody knows.

"Bobby Lynn, what have you heard about me?"

"I don't know what you mean," she said, but she
didn't look me in the eye.

"Does Cecil know, Bobby Lynn?"

"Know what? Now, listen, Tiny, don't get yourself all worked up before you go on."

My mind was racing. Who told? Was it Beau or Luther? No, they would never tell something like that about their daddy. And Mama sure wouldn't tell anybody. Then it had to have been Vern or that grubby preacher. It must have been Reverend Altizer. It was a piece of gossip he just had to repeat. That slimy worm!

"Oh, God, Bobby Lynn, this is awful."

I buried my face in my hands.

"Everybody knows," I said.

"Nobody knows anything," Bobby Lynn said and she put an arm around me.

I couldn't help myself. I looked out the curtains at the audience. The auditorium was overflowing. Hundreds and hundreds of people. And every single one of them knew what Vern did to me.

The hillbillies were heckling somebody onstage again, and I saw Mr. Norse trying to quiet them, but he was getting nowhere. What if they heckled me? What if all the babies started crying while I was singing?

My knees began to tremble. What if I get out there and collapse? What if I forget the words to my songs? What if I open my mouth to sing, and belch instead right into the microphone?

"Shut up!" I said to myself.

But myself would not shut up.

What if my bra strap slipped and showed? Or my half slip fell off? What if . . . ?

My God, it was Jesse! Jesse Compton was sitting out there in his air force uniform! He didn't even tell me he was coming home. He was so handsome, and he was with Connie Collins. I could have died.

"Oh, Bobby Lynn, Jesse is out there!"

"What! Where?"

Bobby Lynn peeped out.

"He's with Connie," I said.

"That weasel!" she said. "Don't you dare let him upset you, Tiny. He's not worth it."

Jesse must know by now, I thought. And Connie. Everybody.

My mouth went dry.

"I wish I could help you, Tiny," Bobby Lynn said sweetly.

"Just find me a place to be alone for five minutes?" I said.

"But your act is coming up. Calvin is going out now. You're after him."

"Just two minutes, Bobby Lynn, please."

"Okay."

Bobby Lynn looked around frantically. The only place available was the dressing room, which was hardly more than a closet, and it was full of girls.

"Please, please move out for just a minute!" I heard Bobby Lynn tell the girls while I stood there clinging to the curtain and shaking in my shoes. "Please let Tiny come in here for just a minute!"

"What for?" they grumbled.

"To pray!" Bobby Lynn said quickly. "It's an emergency. Her act is coming up, and she has to pray."

"Well, all right."

So they moved out of the dressing room and I moved in.

"I'll knock when it's time," Bobby Lynn said and closed the door.

With my heart flying and my breath coming in short, choppy gasps, I wasted no time. I sank to my knees and whispered, "Willa, Willa . . ."

On the wall facing me I read, "Kilroy was here," and I could smell sweat and dirty hair instead of Willa's honeysuckle. But she was there—sort of. I could see her face and part of her hair, which was floating around her almost like the air was liquid. And her face came and went in the dim, smelly room.

"Willa, help me . . ."

"Sing 'I'll See You in the Spring,' " she said softly.

"But we didn't practice that one," I said.

"Sing 'I'll See You in the Spring' after 'The Wayward Wind,' " she said emphatically, and her face faded away.

"Okay, Willa . . . ?"

"Sing only to me," she said as her voice went away from me toward the ceiling.

Bobby Lynn knocked.

"And, Tiny," the fading voice went on, "remember to say nice things to yourself like Aunt Evie told you."

Then I hurried out.

" 'The Wayward Wind,' then 'I'll See You in the Spring,' " I said to Bobby Lynn as we moved toward the stage.

" 'I'll See You in the Spring'! But, Tiny, we didn't practice that one."

"Please, Bobby Lynn, just do it, okay?"

"Okay, 'I'll See You in the Spring' it is!"

"Tiny Lambert!" the emcee was saying.

Everybody applauded politely as I stepped out on the stage with Bobby Lynn. For the first time that night, total silence settled over the auditorium. Not a baby was crying, nor was there a cough or a jeer. I had their attention. Bobby Lynn began her introduction to "The Wayward Wind."

"Tiny," I said in my head, "you can outsing anyone here."

I swallowed hard and began to sing, faltering at first, and still shaking. But as my voice picked up strength, all the tension left my body.

When I finished, the audience applauded enthusiastically.

"You're the best, Tiny!" I said to myself as Bobby Lynn played an intro to "I'll See You in the Spring."

Then I sang to Willa just like she told me.

> *I'll see you in the willow*
> *Weeping in the stream.*
> *I'll see you in the newborn fawn*
> *Soft as in a dream . . .*

And as I sang I saw me and Willa picking daisies and rolling in the grass . . . playing on the high porch and learning to sing . . . Willa drying my tears as we met again during those wee hours two years ago . . . creating a fantasy world to ward off despair during that wet, gray summer . . . Willa dancing in the moonlight and Willa silhouetted in my window while I cried over Jesse.

> *Aromas in the April night*
> *Will steal upon the air;*
> *Twining round about me*
> *Like ribbons from your hair.*
> *I'll hear the whisper of the wind*
> *Like songs you used to sing.*
> *And though you won't be there,*
> *I'll see you in the spring.*

The applause startled me out of Willa's spell. It was thunderous. There was a stomping and cheering and pounding that pulsed through me like drums. It was the sweet sound of approval. They were all standing.

I smiled and bowed slightly. Bobby Lynn came up beside me grinning from ear to ear.

"You're a hit!" she said.

We left the stage, but the applause went on and on.

"Encore?" Bobby Lynn said to Mrs. Miller, our sponsor, who was standing there smiling at me and applauding, too.

"No, no encores in a contest," she said. "But you can take another bow, Tiny."

So I walked out again, and the applause swelled again. This time I saw Cecil clearly with Mama, Phyllis, Roy, and Rosemary, smiling broadly, all of them. Behind them the hillbillies were clapping louder than anybody else, and behind them was Jesse. He was standing there clapping and looking at me with a very serious look on his face. Connie was hanging on to his arm, frowning. She wasn't clapping.

Thirty minutes later the contest was over, and I heard my name called as the winner. The applause started up again. This time I saw that Mama was crying, and I started crying, too.

For some reason a cold October morning flashed into my mind. Frost was shimmering on the mountains and I was riding up a deserted street at dawn, thinking, *I survived!*

# TWENTY-EIGHT

⋟ The next morning, Phyllis and I spread all my prizes around the living room on the couch and chairs. Besides the cash, I had won gift certificates to nearly every store in town, a set of luggage, a watch, a radio, a set of tires, jewelry, spray cologne (Emeraude by Coty), and lots of candy and flowers and makeup. Mr. Theodore Collins, who owned the liquor store, couldn't very well offer his merchandise to high school kids, so he chipped in a paid vacation for the winner and a guest to Virginia Beach. It included bus fare, hotel room for four nights, and twelve meals.

"Take me, Tiny," Phyllis pleaded. "Please, please take me."

"I would, Phyllis, but think now, if it was you, who would you take?"

"Mama."

"Right. I'm taking Mama."

"Taking me where?" Mama walked into the room.

"To Virginia Beach."

"Oh no!" She stopped dead still. "Not me! Why, you'll want to take Bobby Lynn or Rosemary."

"No, I want to take you."

"Yeah, Mama. She wants to take you," Phyllis said.

"Why, I wouldn't know how to act," she said slowly, and her eyes went out of focus.

She was seeing herself at the ocean.

"Why, I don't even have a bathing suit."

"Well, I have a gift certificate for the Style Shoppe. You can buy one. We'll both buy one."

Then she smiled.

"Ain't that something?" she said. "Me at the beach? I never have seen the ocean."

"Me neither," I said. "Just think, Mama, we'll be staying in a hotel by the ocean, and we can eat breakfast in a restaurant."

"Breakfast in a restaurant?" She grinned. "Oh, I gotta tell Dixie!"

She ran to the telephone.

"What a mess!" Beau came into the room. "You won all this loot just for singing a song?"

"She sung two songs, and she sounded like Peggy Lee, only better," Phyllis said.

"Huh!" Beau said.

He picked up a sweetheart ring and turned it over and over in his hand.

"This worth anything?"

"About five dollars," I said.

"Huh!"

"Beau's jealous," Phyllis said.

"Jealous of what?" He snorted. "What would I do with a girl's ring?"

"Give it to Sissy Hess!" Phyllis grinned.

"Girl!" he cried. "You better shut up!"

"Does Beau like Sissy Hess?" I said.

"Yeah, he carried her books to the bus one day when it was raining," Phyllis said, then she ducked as he took a playful swing at her head.

"Beau!" I laughed, sensing that he was reaching out to us for friendship again. "That Sissy Hess is cute as a speckled pup!"

Beau grinned, then grabbed me around the legs, and the next thing I knew, we were tumbling on the floor. He started tickling me, and he was so strong I really could not get away from him. Then Phyllis pitched in to help me, and Luther came in to square things up. We were all laughing so hard we didn't hear Mama yelling. But finally I did hear her, and I peeped through all the arms and legs around me, and there was Mr. Gillespie and a pretty woman right there in the room looking at us. I about had a heart attack. They were both smiling.

"Omigosh!"

I pushed my way to the top of the pile.

"Stop it, Luther! That's enough. Hey, Mr. Gillespie. No more, Beau, Phyllis!"

Finally, the young'uns got the message that someone

was watching, and they rolled back and came to a dead halt.

"Hey, Mr. Gillespie," I said again, breathless. My face was hot as an iron.

"Hi, Tiny," he said, laughing. "My wife and I came by for a minute to congratulate you."

"Well, excuse this mess!" I said, as I swept everything off the couch to make room for them. "Sit down."

They sat down. Mrs. Gillespie was a doll come to life, tiny and cute.

"Can I get y'all some pop or coffee?" Mama said nervously.

"Oh, no thanks," they said.

I sat down by Mama on the other couch. The kids were unnaturally quiet. This was a big event to have a high school teacher visit, especially the band director, who was a celebrity.

"As you know, Tiny," Mr. Gillespie said, "my wife attended Mountain Retreat."

"Yeah, you told me."

Mrs. Gillespie smiled at me.

"We enjoyed your singing last night, Tiny," she said. "You will fit right in at M-R."

"Thank you."

"I was an orphan," she went on.

Well, she sure didn't fit the picture of your average orphan. She looked real smart in her spring dress, and a little square hat, gloves, and high-heel shoes. Luther was gaping at her with a glazed look in his eyes.

"When I went to M-R, I had absolutely nothing but the desire to go to college and study music. Somehow

I scraped together my tuition. It was tight, but such fun!" Mrs. Gillespie said. "You have a lot to look forward to, Tiny."

"I know!" I bubbled over. "I'm so excited I can't think straight!"

We were all excited then, and full of good cheer. We relaxed and talked about M-R, and laid plans for corresponding and seeing each other at Christmas for a progress report, and Mrs. Gillespie told me all about the clubs and things to do, the hikes and swimming in the lake and trips to Asheville for movies and pizza. I wondered what pizza was, but I didn't ask. And she talked for more than an hour, while the kids broke the world's record for quietness and good manners. Then Mr. Gillespie had to pull her away.

"The senior prom is tonight!" he told his wife. "And Tiny has to get ready, I'm sure. Who is your date, Tiny?"

"Cecil Hess." I found myself blushing when I said his name.

"Oh, the valedictorian! Nice boy!"

I was breathless with excitement.

Then, as Mrs. Gillespie was saying goodbye to the kids, Mr. Gillespie suddenly put his hands on my shoulders, kissed me on the forehead, and said, "Congratulations, Ernestina."

And he gave me a secret smile.

I caught my breath sharply.

Then they left.

"Things are clicking so good," Mama said with excitement in her voice. "I can't hardly believe it's all for real."

"I know!" I cried. "It's like Christmas, only better! All the good things are happening at once."

"Now we gotta fix your hair for tonight," she said. "You're going to be the belle of the ball."

The telephone rang as we started up the stairs. Phyllis, Beau, and Luther scrambled for it, and Luther won.

"For you, Tiny. It's Jesse."

He dropped that bomb on me and left the hall. Mama was looking at me. I was looking at my knees, which had suddenly gone weak.

"Ain't you gonna talk to him?" Phyllis said.

Mama patted my shoulder.

"Go on, Tiny. Talk to him."

It was like stage fright all over again. Mama herded the kids out of earshot as I picked up the phone with trembling fingers.

"Hello."

"Hello, Tiny. It's Jesse."

"Hi, Jesse. How's everything?"

"Not so good."

"How come?"

"Well, I saw you last night and I heard you sing," he said very softly.

"Was it that bad?" I joked.

"You were beautiful and you sounded beautiful and I fell in love with you all over again."

I felt my cheeks burning.

"And I know, Tiny. I just know you were singing 'I'll See You in the Spring' to me. That was the last thing I said to you before I went to the air force, remember? I know you remember. I could feel you singing to me."

I didn't tell him I was singing to Willa on that one and not even thinking of him right then.

"Did you hear me, Tiny?"

"I heard you."

"We belong together, Tiny. I was a fool to let you go."

Somehow that just didn't ring true. And I was remembering Aunt Evie and her Ward.

"I want to take you to the prom tonight, Tiny."

"I'm going with Cecil."

"I heard. I know you and Cecil are like sister and brother, you always told me that. So I called him and asked him first if he minded bowing out for you and me. He knows how we feel about each other."

"And what did Cecil say?"

"He said, 'Whatever Tiny wants to do.' He said y'all have an understanding where either one of you can change your mind if you want to."

"Did Cecil sound like he was mad?"

"No! You know how good-natured Cecil is."

Yeah, I knew how good-natured Cecil was. A vision of me and Jesse at the prom came to mind. Him in his uniform and me in my blue formal whirling around the dance floor.

"My baby's so doggone fine," I was remembering.

Everybody would look at us.

Then there was Cecil.

"I want to go with Cecil," somebody said, and it was me.

"Hey, I told you, Pea Blossom, Cecil don't mind. It's you and me again, okay?"

"No, Jesse. It's me and Cecil now."

Did I say that?

"What are you saying, Tiny?"

"I wouldn't go to the prom with anybody but Cecil."

"I see."

He didn't have anything else to say.

"Thanks for asking me, Jesse. That means a lot to me."

"I have to go back to Texas tomorrow," he said.

"Well . . ."

"Yeah, right," he said, and cleared his throat. "Goodbye, Tiny."

"Goodbye, Jesse."

And we hung up. There was a way you could call somebody else on your party line by dialing part of his number, then holding down the receiver. So I called Cecil like that. His ring sounded and was cut short. He must have been standing by the phone.

"Hi, Cecil."

"Hi, Tiny."

"Did you buy my corsage yet?"

"Yeah, do you want me to take it back?"

"Heck no! Why would I want you to do that?"

"Aren't you going with Jesse?"

"I told Jesse I wouldn't go to the prom with anybody but you."

"Really?"

"Really."

I heard him let go of his breath. I smiled.

"You're free, you know, Tiny. We had a deal."

"I know. I want to go with you."

"You do? You're not just saying that?"

"Well, I am saying that, but not *just* saying that. I want to go with you."

"Well, the corsage is white with blue trimmings. I hope you'll like it."

"It sounds cool."

"*You're* cool, Tiny Lambert!"

I laughed as happiness bubbled out of me again.

"See you later, alligator!" he said.

"After a while, crocodile!" I replied, laughing.

And I ran up the stairs two at a time.

# TWENTY-NINE

⤷ Cecil and I were beautiful together. Everybody said so. We danced all the slow dances together and didn't want to dance with anybody else at all. We held hands and gazed into each other's eyes like we were discovering each other for the first time.

Everybody watched us and tried to talk to us. People congratulated me for winning the talent show and Cecil for being valedictorian, but we were all wrapped up in being in love. I wondered how I had lived next door to him for all these years and never before seen how wonderful he was.

Later we went to the Miner's Diner, where a special breakfast was prepared for us, but I don't remember what we ate, or if we ate anything at all. Then we drove home in the warmth of April and starlight and each other.

On my front-porch swing at 4:00 a.m. we talked as we had never talked before—about growing up together and all the funny things that happened, and sad things, too. I said I would tell him all the sad things someday when they didn't hurt quite so much, and he laid his finger on my lips and said, "Hush. There will be plenty of time for everything."

And we talked about the coming months—how there was only a few weeks of school left and how we would spend all summer and vacations together, and I would visit him in Charlottesville, and he would visit me at M-R.

Then he said he had always loved me, and I said I believed that somewhere in my heart I had always loved him, too. I only needed to grow up to realize it.

"I sent you a valentine in the third grade," he said. "But I was too embarrassed to sign it."

"That was from you! I still have it!"

And I decided that I would take that old valentine and I would check YES where it said DO YOU LOVE ME? and I would send it to him at the university next Valentine's Day.

"One day," he said, "Luther overheard me on the party line telling somebody I liked you, and he blackmailed me for years!"

"I remember Luther telling me somebody liked me, but he wouldn't say who."

"I actually beat him at checkers one time," Cecil went on.

"You beat Luther!"

"Yeah, but he said if I ever told anybody, he'd tell you what I said."

"Well, now you can tell the whole world!"

Then we kissed good night. And it was the sweetest kiss.

Later, in my bed, I was thinking about this wonderful feeling and just about to fall asleep when it suddenly hit me I felt exactly this way about Jesse and almost the same about Mr. Gillespie.

Aunt Evie had said you can fall in love more than once. It must be true. So how was I supposed to know when it was real?

"Love is more than a feeling," Bobby Lynn's daddy had said.

Well, I thought, with Cecil I won't plan Forever. I'll just take it one day at a time. Maybe everything will fall in place for us.

When daylight streamed into my room, I woke up. A great emptiness was yawning in me where something used to be. What was wrong?

"Willa?" I whispered, but she was not near.

Nessie looked up at me and started wagging her tail.

I leaped out of bed, donned my blue jeans, and headed downstairs with Nessie at my heels. I grabbed the Henry J key from its hook as I went out the door. Nessie jumped in the back seat, and we headed up the holler in the morning sunshine all the way to the top of the mountain.

I was alone on Ruby Mountain for the first time in my life. But Willa would be there. She must be. I called her name, but she didn't come to me. I couldn't smell her honeysuckle, but I told myself it was not yet May. The fruit trees were all in bloom, and wildflowers were everywhere, but Willa's colors and aroma were missing. I went running to the strawberry patch and the spring, into the cabin, and finally to the willow, calling her, but she was not there.

And it came to me: "I'll See You in the Spring"! It was her way of telling me I didn't need her anymore, and she was saying goodbye.

> *Aromas in the April night*
> *Will steal upon the air;*
> *Twining round about me*
> *Like ribbons from your hair.*
> *I'll hear the whisper of the wind*
> *Like songs you used to sing.*
> *And though you won't be there,*
> *I'll see you in the spring.*

"Willa! Willa! Come back!"

But I knew, even as I went running against the sky, that she would never, ever come again.